Let Me

(McClain Brothers: Book 4)

Alexandria House

Pink Cashmere Publishing, LLC
Arkansas, USA

Printed in the United States of America

First Printing 2019

Pink Cashmere Publishing, LLC
pinkcashmerepub@gmail.com

Let Me Free You

Neil McClain is the screw-up, the one everyone hopes will win but expects to lose. He wants to live a better life, one that his late mother would be proud of, but his belief in himself is weak.

Sage Moniba is in need of a major miracle or she'll be forced to give up the only life she's known.

Neil is searching for freedom from the demons of his past.

Sage is in desperate need of help.

Could it be that what each one needs resides in the other?

Prologue

Neil

My eyes were glued to the colorful Sankofa painting hanging on the wall just behind her in vibrant shades of red, green, black, and yellow, with the exception of the egg resting on the bird's back. It was brown. I had memorized that painting in the nine weeks I'd been living and learning to heal in that place. I'd even dreamed about it a couple of times.

Go back and get it. Move forward, but don't forget to bring those left behind with you. Give back. That was one definition of Sankofa, but the one that touched me was: *Learn from your past, and with that knowledge, move into the future.* That definition spoke to me, hit a nerve, convicted me.

"Don't do that. Don't shut down on me, Neil," said Erica Blake, the beautiful eighties film star and lifelong recovering drug addict who now owned and operated the Sankofa Holistic Healing Center.

I focused my eyes on her. She always looked regal in a bohemian way — loose dress, headwrap that barely could contain her long, graying dreadlocks. Her usual uniform. "I'm listening. I heard every word you said. You think I'm ready to leave. I know I'm not. I was supposed to be here twelve weeks and I need all twelve. I know I do."

She shook her head. "You feel safe here, comfortable. Comfort is good, Neil. But true growth comes from daring to leave your comfort behind. Here, we swaddle our clients, make them feel safe, because one can't heal if they don't trust the healer, but like a mother bird, it's time for us to push you out of the nest. *Now* is the time for you to go. Not in three more weeks. I know that, feel it in my spirit."

My eyes found the painting again as I adjusted my body in the soft brown leather chair that matched the one she sat in. There was no desk in her office, no certificates on the wall, but she was one hell of a counselor — kind, patient, gentle, motherly.

Motherly.

I believe that's why I'd grown so attached to her and this place. She reminded me of my mother. *Damn, I'm glad Mama didn't see me fuck my life up like I did.*

Sighing, I said, "I don't want to...fail. What if I get back out there in the world and I can't cope? What if I relapse, start drinking again, gambling again? I messed up so many times before when I was supposed to do better. I mean, I understand why my family never believes in me. Hell, *I* don't believe in me."

She leaned forward, her elbows on her thighs, the layers of gold bracelets on her arms clanging against each other. "*I* believe in you, and you should believe in yourself. Your ancestors survived a transatlantic boat ride that was nothing short of a vacation in Duat, a trip that many *didn't* survive, designed to weed out the weak. Your people lived through slavery and Jim Crow so that you could carry on their legacy of strength. You are strong, Neil, and talented, and when we're talented like you are, we are so sensitive, so easily convinced that we're less than what we are. *You're ready.* You just have to believe it and receive it. And...I'm not throwing you out there alone. You'll be returning once a week for counseling. Did you not hear that part?"

"I did. I just..."

"You'll be fine. You will. Just remember what I told you."

I chuckled. "You've told me a lot since I've been here. You know that, right?"

"What did I tell you about your power?"

I lifted my eyes to meet hers, straightened my posture, and said, "I am a king, a *black* king, and inside me rests the power of every black king who came before me. It's how I choose to use my power that will either bring me victory or defeat."

She smiled and nodded. "Asé, Neil."

I returned her smile, rubbed my hand down my face, and replied, "So it is, Mother Erica. So it is."

1

Neil

"Damn! You sure you ain't Nolan?! Man! You look good! No wonder you didn't want any visitors. We thought you was in there detoxing and getting group therapy and shit, but what you were really doing was getting facials and massages and pedicures," Everett said, as he stood by the passenger side of his SUV outside the healing center.

I stepped up to him and slapped his hand, smiled when he pulled me into a hug and smacked me on the back.

"Man, ain't been nothing but hard work going on, but it was worth it," I said, stepping back a little.

"It looks like it paid off. You ready to roll? Hey, Chink! Come grab Neil's bag!"

Holding up a hand, I said, "I got it, Ev."

Everett looked at me and nodded. "A'ight. You can throw it in the back and we'll bounce."

We made small talk as Chink drove us to my place. Well, the conversation was actually pretty one-sided with Everett catching me up on what was going on in his world. He shared the success of the *Mrs. South* EP, which had already gone double platinum. That was crazy in a time when folks could download a single cut with ease. But it was a good body of work that I couldn't believe I'd contributed to in the fractured frame of mind I was in at the time. I wasn't perfect after treatment, but I was a hell of a lot better off than I was before.

"I bet Lena has really gotten big," I said, after he filled me in on the video shoot for *Panty Gag*.

"Man, let me tell you. I think my baby girl is gonna be tall like me. She's growing like a weed!"

"Nat and Ella ain't jealous, are they?"

"Naw, Ella is obsessed with Lena. If she could, I think she'd move in with us just so she can hold her all the time. And you know Nat; she goes with the flow. She loves her little sister and is taking this big sister thing real serious."

"That's what's up."

I'd been so damn preoccupied, talking to Everett while fighting my fears about leaving the center at the same time, that I didn't notice we were in Calabasas until Chink was punching the gate code into the keypad at Everett's place.

"I thought you were taking me home?" I said, my eyes on my big brother.

"This is still home for now. Look, I'm proud of you for getting help, but I wanna keep an eye on you for a while. If I like what I see, you can go to your crib."

I wanted to curse him out, tell him I was damn near thirty-seven years old and that I needed my space, that one of the things that kept me from losing my fucking mind during the early days of my treatment was knowing the end result would be me getting my old life back, my independence, but I got it. He'd been out of a lot of money paying off my gambling debts and missed a lot of sleep worrying about me. He was afraid I'd relapse, fall back into my old ways, and since I shared the same concerns and knew beyond a doubt that it was all love on Everett's part, I simply said, "Okay."

"Now, look...I know you don't wanna stay here anymore, but that's the way it's gotta be."

"I feel you, Ev. It's all good."

"No, you are not going back to your house yet. I don't care what you say. I'm your damn big brother, and I'm tryna take care of your ass."

"Ev, I said it's cool. I'm good with staying here."

"For real?" he asked, his forehead full of lines and creases.

"Yeah, I know you're just looking out for me. Am I in the same room?"

"Uh...yeah. Yeah, same room." Everett sounded and looked confused as hell, but I understood that, too. He expected me to fight him on this, but I wouldn't. I was determined to make this life thing work, to straighten my shit out for good, and if that meant being held captive for a minute, so be it.

"A'ight," I said, as I opened the door and hopped out of the backseat. "I'ma head on up to my room and take a nap. Tell Jo I'll catch her later."

"Uh, okay?" Everett called after me as I hopped up the front steps of his house.

*****

"You need to bring your ass down to dinner."

I shot up in the bed, blinking and squinting, trying to figure out what the hell was going on and where I was. "Huh?"

"I done called your ass, texted you, beat on this door, and your ass still up in here sleep? I'm hungry and Jo don't wanna eat until you join us."

The heavy fog of sleep began to lift, and I recognized the bedroom and my brother but still only managed to say, "Ev?"

"Yeah, nigga! Come on so we can eat."

I dragged my hand down my face, nodded, and yawned. "Okay, give me a minute."

As he left the room, he mumbled, "Don't take too long."

Stretching my eyes, I caught a glimpse of myself in the mirror, and muttered, "Shit...so it is."

After I hit the toilet and washed my hands, I trotted down the stairs, and my heart hopped into my damn throat when a crowd of voices shouted, "Welcome home, Neil!"

Everyone was there taking turns hugging me—Ev, Jo, their three girls, Nolan, and his wife, Bridgette. Kim and Leland were missing, but I knew he was on the road with the Cyclones, and Kat and Tommy were with them since Tommy was still running Leland's security and Kat was still Leland's assistant.

"Wow, thank y'all. I mean...damn," I said, too shocked to say much else.

"Well, come eat!" Jo invited me, and then the thought hit me that this was probably her idea. Jo was real sweet, had always been cool to me. Everett was lucky as hell to have her. All my brothers were lucky in the love department, and as I sat down to eat the fancy dinner Everett's cook prepared, I pushed the thoughts of loneliness that eased into my mind away and let myself experience something I hadn't received from my family in a long time—acceptance.

2

Sage

Get up and come get something to eat, sis.

Bridgette's words bounced around in my brain as I rolled over in the bed and buried my face in the downy pillow. I didn't want to move. I didn't want to eat. Truth be told, I didn't want to do anything but lie in that bed and waste away. I was already homeless, sleeping in my friend's guest room. And soon, I'd be country-less, forced to return to a land I knew nothing about. My damn heart was broken in so many ways I'd lost count, and I was just...tired. So tired.

"I'm not hungry," I muttered.

That was a lie. I was *always* hungry. That was why I was skirting the borders of thick and skidding into pure old fat.

"Girl, get your ass up and come on. You know you got that wedding to work today."

I sprang up in the bed. "Shit! What time is it?"

"Time for you to get out of that bed!"

Through a groan, I threw the covers off my body and climbed out of bed. After a trip to the bathroom, I joined Bridgette and her husband for a breakfast of crepes and omelets that I knew had to come from some restaurant, because Bridgette could cook but hated to. I wasn't sure of Nolan's culinary skills. I could cook but wasn't in the right frame of mind to.

As I ate, my eyes darted around the sunny breakfast nook. This house was so pretty. Hell, Malibu was pretty, and the rent-free room was great. I was grateful to the McClains for taking me in after Gavin's ass bailed on me, leaving me with that high-ass rent to pay alone, the rent on the apartment *he* chose, in the same neighborhood where *his* no-keeping-a-job ass's rich parents, who footed his portion of it, lived. He was stupid, but so was I for giving up my reasonably-priced apartment to move in with him after only knowing him a month. But that was me — impulsive, always falling in love — actually, lust — too quickly, gullible, needy, dumb as all hell. And soon to be added to the list? Suicidal, because I truly didn't know how I'd cope with having to leave the only life I'd ever known.

After I cleaned my plate, I left the table and showered. About thirty minutes later, me and my heavy makeup case were out the door.

Neil

I met Emery Tatum Bledsoe in junior high school. She was pretty, tiny, like four-eleven back then and never grew past five-feet-even. She was a true country girl, green as a damn shamrock, innocent as hell, and she was crazy about me from jump.

I was wild. Not the kind of wild that gets arrested for stealing shit or driving drunk or smoking dope. Well, I smoked my fair share of dope back in the day, but what I'm trying to say is, my wildness was more in my thinking. I loved to challenge myself. I liked adventure in every part of my life, especially my sex life, made a game of fucking as many women as I could until I eventually fucked me and Emery up. Because her being my girl and having been my girl for years had no bearing on how many pussies I dipped in. She never complained, never got mad, never said or did anything about it...until she did. And then she left me.

For good.

Shit, she left me and never turned back, completely erased me from her life.

That's when I lost it. I couldn't cope, didn't understand how I could lose my sure thing, my constant, *my heart.* But I did. *I lost her.* She left me, moved on, and was happy, I guess. Yeah, she was happy. She built this great life while I slowly tore mine down punishing myself, I suppose. Drinking to numb the pain of being a habitual fuck-up, gambling just to feel the high that came from winning. But not fucking. I couldn't bring myself to do that. I hadn't had sex in years. Maybe that was part of my self-imposed punishment, too, or maybe I'd fucked enough when I was fucking to never have to fuck again. Or, it could be that my dick just didn't work for anyone but Emery Tatum Bledsoe.

*****

"No, I want the screen to be going the whole time with the graphics and shit. Nonstop," Everett said, irritation on one hundred. I was sitting in with him at a meeting with his stage manager. Courtney, his assistant, was there, too.

"Oh, that's new. So, you want the graphics to be going behind you at all times and the side screens to focus on you? Last tour, you wanted all three on you," Don, a geeky-ass light-skinned dude, said. He'd been Everett's stage manager for years, and they were good friends, but something was going on with my big brother that had zapped his patience.

"That was last tour. This is now. I wanna change it up." Everett scrubbed a hand down his face and stared at the papers covering his desk. "This tour is packed." Falling against the back of his seat, he added, "Shit."

"Yep, just the way you like it," Don said proudly. "We got it all booked in record time, too. The fans are going to go crazy with this many dates to choose from."

Everett closed his eyes and nodded. "Yeah. Uh, I think that's it. Thanks, Don."

Recognizing that he was being dismissed, Don grabbed his briefcase and said goodbye before leaving, a confused look on his face.

"What the hell is going on with you, Ev? You are in a mood!" Courtney said, echoing my thoughts.

My brother shrugged. "I'm good. We got anything we need to discuss?"

"Uh...yeah. We need to really get on looking for my replacement." Courtney had put in her notice so that she could dedicate more time to her husband and new baby. Being an assistant to a rap legend and movie producer didn't fit with her life anymore. It was too demanding and time-consuming, required too much travelling. I knew that from experience.

"Uh, I'm sitting right here," I said. I hated this assistant shit, but he'd put it on me, so I accepted it. Probably would've accepted any role Everett assigned to me. I owed him more than I could ever repay.

"Naw, I'm cutting you loose, letting you get back to your real life," Everett said, his attention on me.

My eyebrows shot up. "So, you letting me go home?"

"I ain't say all that."

"Shit."

"But I'm handing the reigns of your store back over to you. Got some folks interested in your song-writing skills, too. It's time for you to get back on your grind."

"For real?" I asked, surprised and excited as hell at the same time.

"For real. Anyway, go ahead and put the word out or whatever you need to do. See who you can find for me," he said to Courtney.

"Okay. No young females, right?"

"Yeah. That's Jo's rule. Shit, see if you can find a gay man or something. That'd thrill her ass, and that way, I won't have to worry about some dude pushing up on her."

I had to laugh at that. He was not trying to mess up his happy home.

He and Courtney wrapped up their business, and after she left, I said, "So, you gonna tell me what's got you being an asshole to Don? That's your boy!"

"Man..."

"Ev, you don't have to go on this tour if you don't want to. You've done enough."

"Humph, tell that to my bills."

"Nigga, ain't you a billionaire? Your bills are good!"

He sighed.

"Look, I know this has been your way of life for a long time—work, work, and more work—but you been at it since you were a kid, trying to take care of everyone. You ain't gotta do that no more, Ev. Leland is stable. Nolan is stable. Shit, quiet as it's kept, Nole's ass probably richer than you at this point."

Everett chuckled. "The way he is with money? You ain't lying."

"Kat's got Tommy, her business, that little security firm Tommy's starting up. Plus, they're both on Leland's payroll now."

"Yeah..."

"And I'm good. I know you don't believe me, but I am. You don't have to do this tour."

"It's already booked, Neil."

"But have the dates been announced?"

His brow wrinkled. "No."

"Then unbook it! You don't have to do the tour. You don't have to do shit but be with Jo and the kids. I know that's what you really want. You been talking about retiring soon anyway, haven't you?"

He fixed his eyes on me for a minute or two before smiling. "When the fuck did you become the sensible one?"

I chuckled. "I've always been the sensible one, Ev. My sensibility was just hidden under gallons of liquor and mountains of bad decisions."

He nodded. "Thanks for the talk, Neil. I'ma think about it, run it by Jo. She and the babies were supposed to come on tour with me so we could do some of the *Mrs. South* songs, too, but I ain't really with putting her through all that. I don't know..."

"I know you'll do what's best for her. That's your thing — taking care of the people you love."

"I try."

I stood to leave. "You do more than try. Way more."

"Aye, you good for real, though?" His voice stopped me in my tracks.

I smiled and nodded. "Better than I've been in years."

3

Neil

Damn, I missed this place.

I could still remember when I shared this dream-come-true with Everett, way back when I was in college. There was a bookstore around the corner from the Romey U campus — Henley's Books. It was black-owned and housed stacks and stacks of rare books. I might've been a fuck-up, but I'd always loved reading. I told Everett that was my dream — to own a bookstore, and eventually, he made it happen.

"Welcome to Kitabu! How may — oh! Mr. McClain! I wasn't expecting you! It's been a while. Wow! You look good!" Jennifer gushed. She was a college student just like all my other employees were. Look at my ass, talking about *my* employees when Everett still held the deed to the place, just in case.

I gave her a smile. "Thank you. Just popping in to see how things are going."

"Things are going great! Of course, Jackie would know that better than me, but she's off today."

Jackie was my manager, had worked at the store since it opened ten years earlier, and was now working on her PhD. "That's fine. I talked to her the other day."

"Oh, yeah! She mentioned you saying you'd be more hands-on with this place soon."

"Yeah, that's the plan. Well, I'll leave you to it."

She smiled at me and nodded, and I left the store, my

footsteps lighter than they'd been in a long time. Maybe Mother Erica was right. Maybe I *could* do this, have my old life back.

Maybe I wouldn't fuck things up this time.

Sage

I sat on Jo's nice sofa, my eyes on the huge painting of her and Big South that hung on the wall. I wasn't sure what I felt in that moment. Acceptance? Resignation? It wasn't sorrow, for sure. I'd already phased out of anger. This was unfair, but the high-priced lawyer Jo was walking to her front door hadn't said anything more than what I already knew. Of the ways to get a green card, marriage was the most efficient and the quickest. Efficient. I smiled at his usage of that word. He also told us that I wasn't eligible for employer sponsorship, because one: I didn't have an employer or even the prospect of an employer. And two: I would have to possess some vital skill or be indispensable. The employer would have to vouch for the fact that they couldn't find a US citizen to fill my shoes. I did makeup. That was my one and only skill, so…

I sighed, shifting my eyes from the painting to Bridgette, who sat across from me in an accent chair, her eyes on me. She looked so concerned, sympathetic.

"I'm straight, Bridgette," I lied. "It's whatever."

"No, you're not, and that's okay. This is a fucked-up situation that you didn't create. Motherfucking Donald Trump…"

I chewed on the side of my lip to keep from crying. I was so damn sick of crying. "I…"

"I've got it! You're gonna marry one of the bodyguards, and you guys can live in the guest house," Jo announced, once she made it back into the living room and plopped down on the sofa next to me.

"Damn, that's actually a good idea!" Bridgette chimed in.

"But which one? Chink is already married," Jo mused.

"He is? When does he ever see his wife?" Bridgette asked.

"Girl, get this…she's a bodyguard, too. They have the same schedule and hook up on their off days."

"She must be huge! Who does she work for?"

Jo shrugged. "That Paré chick, I think."

"Aw, shit. She and Paré probably fucking, then."

"Oh, they probably are! Back to the issue at hand…Oba's married but separated…"

"Damn, really?"

"Yeah. Uh, Black? I think he's single. I can check with Ev about him and—"

I stood so quickly, I think I startled my friends, because they both jumped in their seats. "You don't have to do this."

"But I want to," Jo said. "We can pay them to marry you."

I chuckled dryly and shook my head. "I'm not that desperate, Jo."

But I *was*.

Her brow furrowed. "I'm not trying to insult you. I just wanna help. I want you to stay here with us. This country is your home."

I looked at her, then swung my eyes over to Bridgette as they filled with tears. "I know, and thank you, but…it's okay. It really is."

But it really *wasn't*.

I left with my friends on my heels, begging me to stay. I probably should've stayed, but I couldn't. I couldn't breathe in that big, spacious house. I couldn't think straight with so much weighing on me. I needed to get out of there if only to sit in my shitty little Toyota and stare into space. But more than anything, I needed to accept my fate, to let my friends off the hook, and to just...cry.

*****

"Where've you been, and why haven't you been answering your phone?! I was about to file a missing person's report!" Bridgette yelled into the phone. And she called *me* loud? "I haven't seen or heard from you in like three days! Where've you been staying? A hotel?"

"I needed to clear my head, and I wasn't going to be able to do that in your house with you and Jo plotting my escape. I appreciate y'all helping me, but it is what it is, Bridge, and I'm okay with it. I've tried everything. I did the best I could. I'll just go to Liberia and make a life there and things will be fine. My parents are going back there soon, so at least I'll have them, and I'll get to meet some of my relatives I've never met. Shit, the food is gonna be lit for sure, and who knows? Maybe the man of my dreams is there."

"Are you serious? I mean, you've been so upset about this, and now you sound like you're good with it."

"I'm not necessarily good with it; I just know it's inevitable, and I'm trying to look at the pros rather than the cons. Pro: African men are fine."

"With big dicks."

"The *biggest* dicks. That's pro number two. Pro three: the climate will be great for my skin. Pro four: I'll get to eat my mom's cooking all the time since I'll probably be living with my folks. Pro five: I'll finally get to see my homeland. I've always wanted to, but just to visit..." Those last words caught in my throat and made my voice quiver. I was totally the-fuck not okay with this, and now Bridgette knew.

"Sage, Jo and I figured this out. Can you come home so we can talk about it?"

I took a deep breath, released it, and blinked furiously to keep the tears at bay. Then I focused on the outside of the boutique I was parked in front of. I was getting ready to go in there and beat the owner's face in preparation for a commercial shoot. The thought of painting on her pretty canvas made my pulse jump. Then I scanned the outside of the building, noting the palm trees that surrounded it, closed my eyes, and breathed in the not-so-fresh LA air that flowed through the open car window. This was home, and I loved it here. I had good friends, and I made good money doing what I loved. I didn't want to leave, would honestly do anything to stay, even marry one of those gigantic-ass bodyguards of Jo's.

So I said, "I'm headed to see a client. Be home in a couple of hours."

My eyes rounded Nolan's and Bridgette's living room, focusing on my friends' faces. "Are y'all serious?"

Jo nodded. "Yes. Dead serious."

With a confused frown glued to my face, I dropped my eyes to my lap. "Well...does he know about this?"

"Neil? Yes, of course he does." Jo said.

"And he's okay with it? I mean, he said he'd do it?" I asked.

"Yes, Sage. We wouldn't be telling you about it if he hadn't. If you're willing, he's willing. That's what he said."

I raised my eyes again. "Why?"

Jo smiled at me. "Because his big brother asked him to do it, and because he wants to help."

"He said that?" I asked. "That he wants to help?"

Jo nodded.

"Wow, I don't know what to say. You guys are serious?"

Marrying a bodyguard was one thing, but marrying a McClain? That had never crossed my mind, but it was a freaking dream come true. Neil was fine as hell. Nolan's twin, but with an edge to him. I preferred thugs, even fake ones like Gavin, but Neil could definitely get it if we had a real, organic relationship which this would definitely not be. That thought doused my spirits. My friends had men who loved them, married them for that reason. I was getting a pity husband. Par for the course for me.

"You just asked that, and again…yes, Sage! We're serious, and we've got it all planned out. I know you always talked about having a big wedding, so that's what you're going to get," Bridgette said.

"Ev and me are gonna handle the cost," Jo interjected.

Bridgette nodded. "And I'm planning the wedding week festivities. Nolan's footing that bill."

With wide eyes and an overwhelmed brain, I asked, "When would we do this?"

"In two weeks," Bridgette said.

My mouth fell open. "Y'all can pull this off in two weeks?"

"With Ev's money? Yeah!" Jo said.

I reclined on Bridgette's sofa, my mind racing with thoughts. Where would I live? With Neil? Were we going to really pretend to be married or would we do the wedding thing then he'd disappear? Was Big South paying him to do this? Did it matter? What would my parents think? Did I really care? It wasn't like I'd made them proud with any of my other life choices, but they'd never said anything about it. I just knew they expected more from me.

"Sage?" Jo's voice was light, soft.

"Uh…" I said.

"I know this isn't what you want. I know you wanted to be in love when you got married. I know you wanted to be able to find another way to stay in the states, but this is what we have. Neil's sweet, and as an added bonus, he's sober. And as another bonus, if you marry him, we'll all be sisters. He's got a great house, and he won't bother you. He won't hurt you. Ev will break his neck if he does," Jo assured me.

I had to laugh at that.

"Girl, please say you'll do this so things can get back to normal. Your ass has not been yourself. I want my loud, crazy, uncultured friend back!" Bridgette pleaded. "I can't deal with Liberian Sage whose subjects and verbs agree and who controls the volume of her voice. You haven't dropped it low since you've been living here!"

I rolled my eyes. "I should be insulted, but I'm not. Okay, I'll do it, but...can I talk to him? I need to hear him say he really wants to do this for my own peace of mind."

"That can definitely be arranged," Jo gushed, and then both of my friends attacked me with hugs.

4

Neil

Two days earlier...

"Marry—what's her name again?" I asked, my forehead wrinkled as Nolan and Everett stood over the weight bench I was sitting on.

"Sage, man! Sage Moniba. You know who we're talking about. The chick that does Jo's makeup," Everett said. "She and Jo and Bridgette are real tight."

I dragged a towel down my face, trying to recall who this chick was. Then I remembered. "The little thick one? Loud as hell? She's Liberian?"

"Yeah, that's her. Look, man...if you do this, I'll consider it a personal favor. Bridgette is so worried about her getting deported, I can't get no sex." Nolan was serious about this, too. For real serious.

"Nole, really? That's what this is about? You want me to marry a motherfucker I don't know so you can get back in your wife's panties?"

Nolan nodded. "Basically, yeah."

Everett shook his head. "Don't listen to this fool. Look, Neil, she's good people. Real sweet. Been in the states since she was little. This is the only home she knows."

"She ain't got a man?" I asked.

"Not anymore," Everett said.

I sighed, rubbed my eyes, and dropped my head. "Look,

y'all…I understand this is a bad situation for her, but can't she find someone else? I mean, shit, anyone else but me?"

"Don't you think she tried?" Everett answered.

"I don't know her other than seeing her hang with Jo and Bridgette. I just got out of fucking rehab. Hell, I'm still in counseling. You think it's a good idea for me to enter into a fake marriage right now? Especially with a loud, ratchet chick? I mean, she's cute, but really? You *want* me to start drinking again?"

Everett scratched his chin. "I think it'd be good to help someone who needs it. Look, Neil…she ain't that bad, and she's from the motherland. I thought you'd be down to help her just for that reason alone, Hotep Howard."

"Man, fuck you."

Everett snickered.

"Where we gonna stay? Here? She moving into my room upstairs?"

"No, you got a house."

"Ohhh, so I get to move back home if I marry her?"

"Yeah. You want your life back? This is how you can get it. I'll even sign your store and house back over to you."

"That's fucked up, Ev. This is fucking blackmail."

Everett shrugged. "Jo asked me to run this by you. She's tryna help her girl."

"And you'll do anything for Jo, won't you?"

"That's my heart. Listen, Jo was thinking about hooking her up with one of the bodyguards, but they all got wives or crazy-ass girlfriends. Then she thought about you, figured it'd be better to pull her into the family anyway, keep her close. That way we'll know she's good."

I hopped up from the bench. I wasn't done with my workout, but I was damn sure done with this crazy-ass conversation. "Sorry, man. I can't do it," I said, and then headed upstairs to shower. An hour later, I was heading out the door to my counseling session with Mother Erica.

*****

It was a night of tossing and turning, my will, mind, emotions, and destiny battling each other so viciously that I finally climbed out of bed and headed down to the kitchen around 3:00 AM. I was sitting at the table with a cup of coffee, reading a book on African spirituality that Mother Erica had suggested, when Everett came into the kitchen.

"What you doing up so early, or late, or shit, whatever it is right now? Lena wake you up, too?" he asked, as he opened the refrigerator.

"She ain't sleeping through the night yet? Ain't she like eight months old now?" I responded.

"Nine. And she sleeps through the night, but her little ass pops up before the sun rises, ready to play. That's my baby, though."

"And she looks just like you. Jo didn't have nothing to do with that."

As he poured a glass of orange juice, he said, "True, true, except for that gap in her teeth and her hair."

"Yeah...but, uh, she didn't wake me up. Couldn't sleep."

He fell into a chair across from me at the table. "You all right? I mean, you good?"

"Yeah...you wanna do a breathalyzer or something to be sure?" I was being an asshole, but damn, I was tired of no one trusting me despite the truth of me not being trustworthy. Hell, I didn't even trust my damn self.

"Just checking."

"Yeah, look...I'll do it. I'll marry ole girl."

He was about to chug that juice but stopped and lifted his eyebrows at me. "You will? What happened in the last less-than-twenty-four hours to change your mind?"

I shrugged. "Had a change of heart."

"You for real? You not just fucking with me, are you?"

"I mean it; I'll do it. I wanna help her. Just tell me where to be and what to do. I'm in."

Everett hopped up and headed out of the kitchen, juice in hand.

"Where you going?" I asked.

"To tell Jo and see if that'll loosen her ass up. She been holding out on me, worried about Sage. I need some pussy."

"You and Nolan ain't shit, you know that?!" I called after him.

He didn't reply or slow his steps.

5

Sage

Now...

So I guess this is when I admit that I'd had a little crush on Neil McClain since first laying eyes on him, even though he didn't have cornrows. It was weird, because I wasn't attracted to Nolan at all, and they were twins. But I guess there was just something about a tortured-ass man that turned me on. It was a horrible trait that'd brought me much heartache in the past if you add to it that when I like a guy, I'm all in from jump. Then factor in that my love affairs are always, *always,* one-sided, and you have the pathetic existence I'd lived nearly since I grew titties. Sage Marjoram Moniba had never heard the words *I love you* sincerely flow from the mouth of a man except for her father. He was such a great guy, really, and he loved me so much. I didn't get why I always chose the wrong men when I had grown up with such a great example, but I suppose your destiny is your destiny, and mine was to be in lop-sided relationships where I did all the giving and the men did all the taking.

Anyway, I had a long talk with myself before this meeting with Neil, told myself that he was doing me a favor, being nice. I was a charity case who couldn't get her real boyfriend to marry her. Did he know that? I really hoped not. That shit was just embarrassing.

He sat across from me in Jo's and Big South's living room,

wearing jeans and a plain white t-shirt with Nike slippers. His eyes were on me, those dark eyes that always looked sad and wise at the same time to me. He had a goatee and mustache like Nolan, but his wasn't as neat as his twin's, and Neil's hair was a little longer than Nolan's, too. If not for those subtle differences, I would've felt bad for lusting after him since he looked like my friend's husband.

"So...you wanted to meet with me?" His deep voice filled the room.

Damn, how long had I been sitting there staring at this man? I really needed to get my shit together. "Huh? Oh...yes! I wanted to thank you and to be sure you were okay with doing this—marrying me, I mean. I know it's a big thing to ask you to do. You don't know me. Not really."

He smiled at me, a smile that reached his dark eyes. "Yeah, I'm okay with it. I wanna do this. I wanna help you."

"Uh...you know we'd have to stay married for at least three years, right? Could take up to five for me to get my citizenship. They told you about that?"

He nodded. "They told me, and I'm good with it."

"Is your girlfriend good with it?"

He frowned a little. "I don't have a girlfriend. I have a fiancée."

"Oh! Is she okay with this? I wouldn't want to mess up your relationship with her."

"*You're* my fiancée, Sage."

"You were talking about me? Shit, I'm dumb."

He chuckled and left his seat, sitting down next to me and making my pulse throb in my neck. Never in my wildest dreams did I ever think I'd one day marry a man like this, a man who was such a...*man*. Built, handsome, smelled divine. Damn.

"I don't have a girlfriend, no relationship. But I'm about to marry what I've been told is a wonderful woman, and I hope, at the very least, we can be friends through all this since we'll be living together."

"Yeah...me, too," I said to his lips.

"So, I hear we're having a big wedding?"

"Uh, yeah, if that's okay with you."

"It is. A Christian ceremony?"

"Well, yeah. Is that a problem?"

"No, but I'll want to make some minor adjustments to the vows. I'm not exactly a traditionalist."

"Oh, that's fine. Um, I want to go with an all-white color scheme. I thought I'd run that by you since I know you're hotep and everything..."

He shrugged. "I'm cool with that. The Creator created all colors. But, uh...you sure you don't want an accent color or something?"

"No, I've always had a thing for the color white. So I don't want any other colors except maybe the groomsmen's ties."

"Okay. I'm with it. So, is there anything else I need to prepare for? Anything special you plan on incorporating into the ceremony?"

With wide eyes, I nodded. "Uh, yeah...I mean, not the ceremony, really, but I wanna do the traditional Liberian entry at the reception. And my dress will be a traditional Liberian one for the reception, too. My mom's gonna get you an outfit to match mine, so I'll need your measurements."

"Okay. Your parents know about this arrangement? They're okay with it?"

I shrugged. "They know how I am, how impulsive I can be. I've always kind of done my own thing. When I told them I was getting married, they assumed I fell in love with you on-sight, because I sort of have a history of doing that, and I didn't bother correcting them, so they're just going with the flow like they always do. Oh! My dad needs to see your house, though. He wants to make sure it's nice and that I'm not marrying a man who, and I quote, 'is a Jack who pumps tires' for a living." I mimicked my father's waning Liberian accent.

Neil chuckled again, and I joined him because my dad was

a mess.

"Okay, no problem. We need to figure out when you're moving your stuff in anyway."

"Right. Uh, Neil? What exactly do you do for a living? My mom asked, and I just said you work for yourself."

"I own a bookstore when Ev lets me own it. And I write music. Those are my main sources of income, but I used to paint and dabble in photography, too. I write poetry from time to time, as well, but I never got paid to do that."

"Okay, so I'll stick with my initial answer."

He laughed. "Uh, you do makeup, right?"

"Uh-huh. It keeps me pretty busy."

"You do your own? You look beautiful."

"I do? I mean, yeah, I do my own makeup. Thank you."

"You're welcome."

"Hey, um…what bills do you want me to pay?"

His eyebrows rose, and he leaned back a little. "Uh…none. I got it."

"You sure? I can pay the mortgage, maybe? My income isn't exactly stable, but I do pretty good."

"Um, my house is paid for, a gift from Ev. I can handle the utilities."

"I can do the groceries, then. I gotta pay my way."

"If you want to…"

"I do." I fell against the back of the couch and shook my head. "We're really doing this, aren't we?"

"Yeah," Neil said, "we really are. So…the kiss?"

I sat up straight and tilted my head to the left. "Kiss?"

"At the wedding. We'll have to kiss. That could be…"

"Awkward?"

"Yeah."

"Right, so maybe we should practice?" I suggested. *Please say you want to practice.*

"That's a good idea. We could practice now."

"All right…"

"Tongue or no tongue?"

"What?"

His eyes were on my mouth as he repeated, "Tongue or no tongue?" Or shit, maybe I imagined him looking at my mouth.

"Uh, no tongue?" I was definitely not ready for tongue. Not ready at all.

He gave me a boyish smile and nodded. "No tongue it is."

Moving in closer to my face, he nearly whispered, "You ready?"

"Uh-huh," I sang softly.

"On a count of three," he murmured. "One…two…three."

His lips brushed against mine so softly that I had to open my eyes and see if he was still there, if it really happened. Then, with his eyes shut, he reached up and grasped the back of my head and kissed me for real. Like, *for-real, for-real*. That tongue of his darted out, my pocketbook started shmoney dancing, and the next thing I knew, we were both moaning into each other's mouths.

What in the whole hell was this?

Whatever it was had me as wet as the English Channel.

Shit! This was some electric, insta-chemistry stuff!

Then he snatched his mouth away from mine, hopped to his feet, and with this wild look in his eyes, said, "Uh, sorry about that." He cleared his throat. "You said no tongue, and I…"

"No—it's okay." *It's very okay.*

"So…you got my number from Jo, right? Just text me and let me know when you want to move in and bring your folks over."

"Ah, all right?" I said, reaching up to rub my lips. *Did I just dream that shit?*

He nodded for probably the twentieth time and left. And I just sat there thinking that maybe I shouldn't marry this man, but at the same time, my vagina said, "Bitch, please."

6

$\mathcal{S}age$

"...and I tell her, you do it? I-will-whip-you-and-you-will-cry!" Four days after Jo and Bridgette dropped the marrying-Neil bomb on me, my father was holding court in Neil's living room as the movers carted my stuff into the house. Neil had directed them to take the boxes to his bedroom for my parents' sake.

I didn't have much to move since I'd left all my furniture at the apartment I shared with Gavin's sorry ass, just clothes and my makeup. But I had a lot of makeup, boxes upon boxes of promo kits and stuff I'd purchased myself. And shoes. I loved shoes. Oh, and perfume. I liked smelling good. In short, I was moving in a bunch of shit.

Neil laughed at my father's attempt to embarrass me. I say attempt, because I barely knew this man anyway, so embarrassing me in front of him was totally impossible.

"So, she was a handful, huh?" Neil asked.

"Aaaayah! I tell you! It's tee trufe!" my dad shouted. "She a biggity one, too! Got dear taste!"

When my father was in his element, his words rushed out so rapidly that I couldn't understand him sometimes. So, I knew poor Neil had to be struggling. "He's saying I'm stuck up and have expensive taste. Neil doesn't know Liberian Koloqua, Papa."

"I speak good English-oh!" my dad declared.

I fought not to roll my eyes, and Neil chuckled. It looked like he was really enjoying this little conversation with my father.

"Aaaayah! *Turn Back tee Hands of Time!*" my father added, garnering a confused look from Neil. I'd have to tell him later that my father quoted Tyrone Davis like he was quoting damn Tennyson or somebody. It was a problem.

"Sage! You hear me! Come here!" That was my mother, acting like she'd been calling my name for years.

I sighed, stood from Neil's leather sofa, and left my father to his performance.

"Yes?" I said, as I entered the gorgeous kitchen full of sleek, stainless steel appliances.

"Help me with this food," she said. While my father lived for moments when he could display his accent, my mother worked overtime to shed hers, although it slipped out at times.

I fell in beside her at the counter, spooning Jollof rice and plantains into Neil's nice white bowls, fufu onto plates, and potato greens into separate bowls.

"He's handsome. *Built*," my mom said.

"He is," I agreed.

"And nice. All those books in that living room? He likes to read?"

I almost asked her how I was supposed to know that, but instead, said, "He owns a bookstore."

"Oh?! He know book, eh?" There was her first slip of the day.

"Yes, he's very smart," I replied.

As usual, that slip led to an avalanche of Koloqua. "He a growna man, dat one. Fine, fine as can be. Too-fine! I see why you marry so fast!"

I couldn't help but laugh at that, and I was still grinning when I called my father and Neil to the kitchen for dinner.

Neil

I felt like I was in the middle of an Afrocentric dream, sitting at a table with people from the motherland, eating authentic Liberian food. *If Sage can cook like this, this shit just might work out in my favor.*

I took a gulp of water and went back in. The food was spicy as hell, but damn, it was so good!

"Neil, my man…you like my Baby's cooking-oh?" Mr. Moniba asked me.

"Samuel, let the man eat!" Mrs. Moniba scolded. "Let him finish before you start asking about the food!"

"He about to be family! Da-me! You know dat! You behind me all tee time for no-ting!" Sage's father complained. *"Mom's Apple Pie!"*

I frowned, wondering if her dad had Tourette's or something. "It's good. Thank you, Mrs. Moniba."

With a huge, proud smile on her face, Sage's mother said, "You're welcome, son."

"Aaaaaye! *In tee Mood!*" her father declared.

As I helped Sage carry her boxes from my bedroom to the guest bedroom, now her room, I said, "I can't believe your mom's first name is actually Baby."

"Believe it. Strange names are a trend in our family. My mom's name is Baby, I'm Sage, and my sister is Ferula. Weird."

"Your parents were into plants?"

"My mom was, still is. She's always had a garden. You know the potato greens we ate tonight? She grew the sweet potatoes for them."

"Wow, really?"

"Yep."

"And your father is a carpenter?"

"Uh-huh. They're both hard-working people, unlike me."

"Nah, I bet you work hard."

She shrugged as I followed her back to my room to grab more boxes. "I guess. I like it, so it never feels like I work hard."

"Yeah."

We were all done moving things to her room, and both just stood there kind of staring at each other until she finally said, "They were impressed with you. My parents, I mean. Thanks for being so nice to them."

"Your folks are cool, so it's no problem. And thanks for explaining the Tyrone Davis thing. I was like, what the hell?"

She giggled. "I know! He needs to stop that mess!"

"Naw, I like your folks. It was fun hanging with them."

"Well, they like you, too. My mom thinks you're fine."

"For real? I'm a'ight, I guess."

"No, you're definitely more than 'a'ight.' I couldn't ask for a finer fake husband."

"Hmm, well...I could say the same thing. You're stunning."

She dropped her eyes and covered her mouth with her hand. "You don't have to say that."

"It's the truth." And it was. Sage was shorter than me and was thick as hell. Big thighs, hips a mile wide. Back in the day, I wasn't really into women built like her, but she had the kind of curves that could make a man lose it. And she wasn't a light-weight. She was built like those women Leland loved to date. She had a little gut on her, but that just added to the appeal to me, knowing she ate like a real woman. I honestly didn't know why I never noticed how attractive she was before, but I guess I was in too deep of a mental hole to see her clearly.

"Uh, thank you."

"You're welcome. I'll leave you to get settled in. Your bathroom's across the hall. Shit, I already showed it to you, didn't I? You know what? I'ma just shut up and leave you alone. You know where my room is, if you need me."

"Yeah, thank you again, Neil. I don't think I can say it enough."

"No problem. Oh, and I'm truly sorry about that kiss the other day."

Her eyes narrowed at me. "Don't be."

7

Sage

Neil's house was an older home located in Venice — LA, only a few blocks from the beach and not far from the canals. It was small, maybe one thousand square feet, and besides the living room, kitchen, and dining room, had two bedrooms, two baths, and a gorgeous backyard garden area. There were padded swings on the front porch that my father had a fit over when he saw them. My parents loved the place when Neil led us on a tour, but then again, it was a beautiful home, and it felt like…it felt like it was *my* home, like I belonged there, and I couldn't understand why. Wishful thinking, maybe? Perhaps I just wanted it to be my home? Or was it that I wanted a home, period, someplace to hang my clothes without fear of having to pack them up again when my relationship inevitably went south.

He gave me his guest bedroom, and I slept better that night than I had in a long time. Possibly, that was because the issue of being deported was now solved, or possibly, it was something else — a serenity that folded itself around me and squeezed me tightly from the moment I laid my head on the pillow. Neil was a tortured soul. He was nice, kind, but he still wore his scars. I could see them in the sadness that lived behind his eyes, so it didn't make sense for the place to feel like such a sanctuary, but it did.

I walked around the small living room that housed a tan leather sofa, matching recliner, and a coffee table shaped like the continent of Africa. My dad had a fit when he saw that, too. Two of the walls held bookcases filled with books, making the space appear even smaller, but not in a claustrophobic way. I stepped over to one of them, running my fingers over the book spines — James Baldwin, Octavia Butler, Cornell West, Michael Eric Dyson, Ta-Nahisi Coates, bell hooks, Dr. Carter G. Woodson, Alex Haley, Dr. Claud Anderson, Baba Ifa Karade, Axsal Johnson, Henry Louis Gates Jr., Isabel Wilkerson. So many books. I wondered if he'd read them all. Then I turned around and scanned the room again — no TV.

"Grand rising."

I jumped at the sound of his voice, so much like Nolan's. In my morning haze, I almost forgot I'd moved out of his and Bridgette's house.

"Hey," I replied, my eyes on his bare chest. Daaaamn. "You were out back?"

He nodded, shifting his body so that he was leaning against the door facing that led into the dining area. "Yeah, meditating. Tryna keep my mind right, stay on the right path."

"You're a Buddhist?"

"Nah, not really. I kind of study all religions. Meditation is a part of all of them in some form."

I'd seen a Quran, a Bible, the Handbook of Yoruba Religious Concepts, and a Tripitaka on one of those shelves, so he was definitely doing some religious research.

"What've you learned?" I asked.

He shrugged, crossing his arms and making his pecs flex. Double daaaamn. "That they all have things in common, and that they all have things I disagree with, other things I agree with."

"Hmmm. Hey, you've read all these books?"

"Not all of them, but I'm working on it."

"You went to college, right? What'd you get a degree in? Reading books?"

He chuckled and smiled, showing off his gorgeous teeth. Triple daaaamn. "No, African American Studies."

I twisted my mouth to the side. "Makes sense."

He chuckled again. "So, today you pick your dress out, right?"

"Yeah, and you get fitted for your tux?"

"Yep."

Then we stared at each other for a minute before I dropped my eyes, because shit, Neil was making me melt right where I stood. What the hell was this?

"Jo and Bridgette picking you up?" he asked.

I lifted my eyes. "Uh-huh."

"You had breakfast yet?"

"No, I don't usually eat breakfast."

"You don't? That's not good."

"I know. I need to do better."

He gave me another smile. "Well, I'ma help you do better. Come on. Let me hook you up."

I returned his smile as I followed him into the kitchen.

*****

"I can't believe how good that egg-white omelet was! And he used this vegan cheese stuff. And that organic apple juice was the damn bomb!" I rambled, as I slid into the one-thousandth dress at Kelli's Bridal Shoppe, a high-end boutique that specialized in plus-size wedding gowns. Those dresses were expensive as hell, but Jo was the one doing the swiping, so I was good with it.

My eyes surveyed my image in the mirror. This dress was

like a fantasy in fabric form. It was a white mermaid gown with a sweetheart neckline, lacy straps, an illusion-style back, and it fit the hell out of my thickness, made me look hot. With a nice updo or my face framed in curls, I'd kill this wedding thing! But since my natural hair was short, that would require a weave or a wig.

I finally stepped out of the dressing room to get Jo's and Bridgette's feedback on the dress and flinched when they both started squealing at the same time.

"You look soooo beautiful!" Jo gushed. "This is the one! This is it! Right, Bridge?"

As Bridgette wiped her eyes, she mumbled, "Fucking defective tear ducts..." Then she sniffled, and said, "I feel like a proud mother. You look gorgeous, Sage. Gorgeous."

With a big grin, I looked at myself in the standing mirror sitting outside the dressing room and nodded. "Yeah, this is definitely the one." That was where I would also say, "Neil is gonna love it," only Neil wasn't marrying me for love, so he didn't care what my dress looked like.

"It sure is. You-you're glowing, Sage, and I'm glad you and Neil are getting along so well. He cooked for you? It's almost like this marriage is a real one," Jo said to my back, as I headed back into the dressing room.

"Yeah," I muttered. She didn't have to remind me of the fact that my life was pitiful and the only husband I could get was a fake one. Those thoughts already stayed in the front of my mind.

Neil

"So you're retiring for real?! Or is this one of them Hov retirements?" I asked, through the dressing room door.

"Naw, this is real. It's time. I put in more than enough work to let it go now. I'ma do some music producing, be more hands-on with McClain Films, get on Jo's nerves being up under her. I'm done with the stage," Everett answered.

"I'm happy for you, man, and you're gonna break records with this abbreviated farewell tour you're gonna do," I said.

"Yeah, five cities, one night each? Those tickets are gonna sell out in seconds," Nolan agreed.

"I hope so," Everett said.

"That's sharp, man. I wasn't sure about the all-white thing, because you know I like a pop of color, but damn, that's niiice," Nolan said, as I stepped out of the dressing room and modeled the tux for him and Everett like a damn chick. Like this was *Say Yes to the Tux* or some shit.

"Thanks, Yves St. Hilfiger. Ev, what you think?"

"It's nice, man. Real nice. That mug is legit."

I looked at myself in the mirror, adjusted the white bow tie, and agreed, "Yeah, I think Sage'll like it, too. She was firm on the all-white theme."

Silence from my brothers.

I turned around to see them giving each other a look. "What?"

Everett, who was stretched out in his chair, shrugged. "Nothing. But, uh, you and Sage really getting along, huh? Y'all talking about the wedding and shit?"

"She lives with me, Ev."

"Nigga, she just moved in with you. You act like she been there for months or something."

"I wasn't finished. She lives with me, *and* we're getting married. I'm not supposed to talk to her? We can't be friends?"

"Oh, shit! Y'all friends? Already?" Nolan asked, with a stupid-ass grin on his face. I didn't care if we were identical. I'd never looked that damn silly in my life.

"Damn, y'all...you want me to hate her or something?" I asked, turning to look at myself in the mirror again. Detoxing, counseling, and working out had me looking fresh as hell.

"Naw…I just didn't expect you to stick your tongue down her throat. That's all I'm saying," Everett said.

"What?!" Nolan shrieked.

I snatched my head around to look at Everett. "What are you talking about? You were spying on us?"

"How in the fuck I'ma spy on you in my own house, nigga?" Everett replied.

"Wait, wait, wait…you and Sage? Y'all fucking?!" Nolan asked, sitting on the edge of his seat. This idiot…

"A kiss ain't fucking, Nole! And we were…we were just practicing for the wedding. You know, so shit won't be awkward."

"Y'all practicing for the honeymoon, too? How was her first night living with you? She practice sleeping in your bed?" Everett asked, with this dumb look on his face. Everett was a damn clown if I ever saw one.

I shook my head. "Y'all asked me to marry her, I'm tryna make the most of it, and you wanna fuck with me about it? Y'all some assholes for real."

"I'm just messing with you, Neil. Hey, thanks again for this, and you know what? If y'all make something real outta this, I'm all for it. Sage ain't a bad catch, and I know she gets bonus points with you for being born in Africa," Everett said.

"I don't know about all that…"

"Hmm, that was one hell of a kiss I saw, though."

As I headed back into the dressing room, I thought, *it sure in the hell was.*

That kiss had me so hard, I damn near ran up out of that living room to keep her from noticing. Shit, I guess my dick worked for someone other than Emery Tatum Bledsoe, after all.

*****

My eyes were tired, but I had so much reading to catch up on. I had so much *life* to catch up on. I'd wasted a lot of years chasing peace in the bottom of bottles, feeling sorry for myself, punishing myself, trying to fix something that was irreparable. I had a lot of catching up to do, period.

The first thing I did when I heard the tapping on my bedroom door was to take off my glasses and rub my eyes. Then I said, "Come in."

The door eased open, and Sage stepped inside just a little bit. My eyes swept up and down her body covered in a tank top and some little shorts. Her skin looked so soft. It'd been a long time...

"Um, I just wanted to say good night. I wasn't sure if you were asleep. Your door was closed when I made it home," she softly uttered.

"Not sleep, just reading. You had a good time dress-shopping?"

"Yeah, I always have a good time with my girls. But I'm tired. It's been a loooong day, because we shopped for honeymoon clothes, too, then we ate and went to Bridgette's and hung out. Um, did you know there was a honeymoon?"

"Yeah...in Palm Springs, right?"

"You're okay with it? The honeymoon, I mean?"

"I'm good with it. I mean, friends can go on a trip together, right?"

"Yeah..."

"And we're friends, or on our way to being friends, right?"

Her eyes rounded the room and then she nodded. "Uh-huh."

"Are *you* good with a honeymoon? If not, we don't have to go. Or you can go alone?"

"No...I'm good with it, but where—what about the sleeping arrangements? I mean..."

"Oh, I think Ev said it was a suite, so if there's a couch, I can knock out on it."

"You sure?"

"Yeah."

"Okay…"

"We good on the honeymoon now?"

Her eyes scanned the room again. "Yeah."

"Good."

She stood there looking like she wanted to say something else, and finally voiced, "I guess I'll go to bed now. Good night, Neil."

"All right. Good night, Sage."

She left, closing the door behind herself and I closed the book and my eyes, sighed, and tried to wipe the image of that unsure expression she always wore around me and the way she'd bite her top lip when she was nervous out of my mind. Because for some crazy reason, all of that was turning me on.

8

Sage

Five days before the wedding...

I unwrapped the hardcover copy of *Sixty-Nine Sexual Positions for Adventurous Couples* and turned it around for the guests to see. "Thanks, Yasmine!" I said to my friend-slash-client with as much enthusiasm as I had when I unwrapped the edible panties I got from Hera, the crotchless panties I got from my cousin Gracie, and the countless pieces of lingerie I got from nearly everyone else — everybody I was associated with was a damn freak! Add all that to the gushing congratulatory wishes I'd been getting since I stepped into the room in McClain Studios where the bridal shower was being held, and I felt like an enormous fraud. Hell, I *was* a fraud. Maybe I should've just taken my ass to Liberia, but I liked living with Neil. I liked being around him, and I liked the fact that I was marrying him. As far as fake husbands go, Neil wasn't a bad catch, and shit, I liked him. Always had — whether he was drunk or sober. Like I said before, when my friends were securing their McClains, I secretly had my eye on the broken one, the one they all felt sorry for, wishing he'd get fixed, and he did.

I opened the last gift, a pink, fuzzy pair of handcuffs, thanked Ellis, one of my long-time clients, and breathed a sigh of relief when everyone took their eyes off me and started refilling their drinks and plates.

"Damn, you racked up on freaky shit. Makes me wish I'd had a shower," Bridgette, who was sitting to my immediate right, said. "You need to donate some of this stuff to me."

I shrugged and mumbled, "Take what you want. It's not like I'll be needing it."

"You got like seven cock rings," Jo, who was sitting on the other side of Bridgette, informed me.

"Oh, I don't need those," Bridgette said.

"Girl, you got enough inventory to open an online sex shop," Jo suggested.

"Damn, I wish those crotchless panties were my size! Shit, I might take that ball gag home, though. See if Nole is into it." That was Bridgette.

My phone pinged, and I was grateful for the distraction. I couldn't help but smile when I saw that the text was from Neil: *How's the shower going? You get us a toaster? A Keurig? Some sheets?*

Me: *Actually, Bridgette gave us a really nice French press. Jo got us a panini maker. Almost everyone else got us freaky stuff, enough to make a small fortune if I sell it.*

Neil: *Why would you sell it?*

Me: *What else am I gonna do with it?*

It took him a full minute to answer me: *Use it.*

What?!?!

Me: *With who?*

"Get off that phone, girl! Break time is over. We got like two more games to play," Bridgette shouted from across the room.

I was so deep in that text conversation with Neil, I hadn't noticed she'd moved away from me.

With a groan, I lifted from my chair and made my way to where she'd set up for the toilet paper wedding dress competition. By the time the shower was over, Neil still hadn't replied to my text.

Neil

"Damn, this really is a lot of shit!" I said, as I brought the last of the shower gifts in from Sage's car.

"Why didn't you respond to my last text?" she asked. She was standing in the living room, her eyes on the pile of presents sitting in the middle of the floor. Something about her shyness around me was so sexy...

"What text?"

Lifting her eyes to mine, she raised an eyebrow. "The one where I asked you who I'm supposed to use this freaky shit with."

"Well, that depends. What kind of freaky shit did you get?"

She shrugged. "A feather tickler, handcuffs, and throat-numbing spray, just to name a few."

"Damn."

"Yeah, I know."

"Uh...Sage?"

"Mm-hmm?"

"Friends sometimes have sex, don't they? I mean, I *know* they do."

Her eyes widened. "You wanna be the kind of friends that have sex? You-you wanna have sex with me?" she squeaked.

This time, I dropped *my* eyes, because this whole conversation was just bizarre and out of line and I didn't even know why I was going there, but I couldn't stop myself. So I said, "Yeah."

"For real?" Her voice was even higher pitched. Her forehead, furrowed.

"Yeah. I'm attracted as hell to you, and we're getting married, gonna be sharing our lives for the next three years at least, and shit, I'm a man. I have needs."

"I figured you weren't going to be celibate this whole time; I just thought you had you a woman you could go to for that."

"Naw, I don't mess around with women who are good with playing second anymore, because as my wife, you'd be first."

"Oh..."

Then a thought hit me. "Wait, you don't wanna have sex with me, do you? Shit, I'm sorry. I just assumed you did, and I don't know why I assumed you did..."

"No! Hell no! That's not it! I wanna have sex with you. I wanna fuck the shit outta your fine ass." She capped that statement by smacking her hand over her mouth.

I grinned at her slip. "You're fine, too." I let my eyes drag up and down her body full of curves. "Yeah, you are absolutely, positively fine."

"You need to stop playing with me. Are you just saying all this shit to fuck with me? To make me feel better about you having to be my mercy husband?"

"Not at all. Sage, I'm woke than a motherfucker. I have dedicated my life to the truth. I hate lies. I'm not lying. I want you in that way, but only if you want me. If you don't, we can keep it platonic. I'm good either way." *Please say you want me, though.*

"Didn't I just say I wanna fuck the shit outta you? I just don't want to be..."

"What? Wait, I don't want you to think I'm tryna use you for sex. It's not like that. This would have to be mutual. You'd have to want this, too."

She shook her head. "I just said I want to! It's not that I think you're using me or trying to use me..."

"Well, what is it, then?"

With her eyes on me, she said, "Nothing."

"No, what is it? Tell me."

She sighed. "It's...I'm just afraid that if I put my body in this, my heart will follow. That's just how I'm wired. It's all...it's connected, and I habitually fall in love, or think I'm falling in love. That would be especially bad in this case, because the thing is, this isn't real. I don't want my heart broken. I've had enough heartbreak in my life already."

"My shit is connected, too, Sage, and my heart has been broken before, broken like a motherfucker. So I'm running the same risk with my heart that you are with yours. And as far as this not being real? We can make it real."

"Seriously?"

"Yeah, seriously. Anything else bothering you?"

"Yeah, um, I mean no, but when will we...when do you wanna start...fucking?"

I chuckled. "Straight to the point, huh?"

She shrugged.

I thought about it for a moment, decided *right damn now* wasn't the best answer, and said, "How about during the honeymoon? We could make it like a real honeymoon, you know?"

She smiled, and her smile was so damn pretty. "Okay."

9

Sage

Four days before the wedding...

Neil: *I'ma fuck you until you scream my name with a Liberian accent.*

Me: *Why do you think I can do a Liberian accent? Because I'm Liberian? That's racist or something.*

Neil: *If you can't do one, my dick is gonna give you the ability to do it. You can call me Superdick.*

Then he texted me an airplane emoji and an eggplant emoji. I giggled under my breath.

Me: *You talking all this shit and I'm tryna find out if you can really handle this young pussy I got.*

Neil: *Who the hell is this? Where's shy Sage at?*

Me: *Shy Sage leaves the building when it's time to get down. That's when Nasty Sage shows up.*

Neil: *I like Nasty Sage. She's my kind of woman. Tell Nasty Sage I'ma eat her like she's a plate of chicken and waffles.*

"Ah!" I shrieked, making both Bridgette and Jo turn around and give me curious looks. They were getting manicures while I soaked my feet. I was into the pedicure stage, having already gotten my manicure. Bridgette wasn't playing with this wedding week schedule. Tomorrow, we were supposed to be going to a luxury hair salon.

"What you laughing at back there?" Bridgette asked.

"Nothing," I muttered. Then I answered his text: *Aren't you vegan, though? Should you be eating meat? Pussy is meat.*

Neil: *I'm actually an ovo-lacto vegetarian, but sometimes I'm a carnivore. I listen to my body. If my body craves fruit, I give it fruit. If it tells me to eat vegetables, that's what I do. Right now, it's telling me to eat pussy. Specifically, your pussy.*

"She's probably on Instagram looking at one of those comedians' videos. You know she lives on IG," Jo said.

Me to Neil: *I sure hope you back up all this shit you're talking.*

Neil: *Just call me Pardison Fontaine.*

Rolling my eyes, I tucked my phone in my purse and watched the pedicurist dry and oil my feet. "Do y'all think me and Neil would be a good match if the circumstances were different?" I asked.

"Shit, y'all are a good match now. You need a husband and he's willing to marry you," Bridgette answered.

"I mean, our personalities and stuff. You think they match?"

"I don't know, Sage. Neil's so quiet most of the time, it's hard for me to get a good bead on him," Jo said.

"But you've been quiet, calmer lately, so y'all might be a perfect match. Y'all still getting along?" Bridgette said.

"Yeah, we're cool." They were my closest friends, but something was telling me not to share the progression of my relationship with Neil with them. Probably because I knew I had no business planning to screw him. But shit, I wanted to.

I really, *really* wanted to.

As Jo started telling us about Everett wanting to sign Nat up for tee ball in the spring, my phone dinged again.

Neil: *I'ma put your titties together and suck both of them at the same time. Ask Nasty Sage how she feels about that.*

Me: *Fuck Nasty Sage. Shy Sage is wet as hell right now. It's like a swimming pool between my legs.*

Neil: *Awww, shit! I can't wait to swim in it. I'ma be Superdick Phelps!*

At that, I cackled out loud but calmed down when both Jo and Bridgette turned to look at me again.

*****

"Get it, Sage! Get it! Yassss! Feel all up on that chocolate, girl!" Bridgette egged me on, as I rubbed the buff stripper's chest and winked at him.

The tall, sexy stripper, whose name was Snoop Dong, flicked his tongue at me and then fell to his knees in front of me, burying his face between my legs and shaking his head from left to right. Screams and squeals filled the private room inside of *The Launch Pad* as I covered my mouth and giggled.

This secret bachelorette party was lit as hell! It was a secret, because if Big South or Nolan had any idea that their wives had hired this stripper to entertain us, they'd both be right here in this room with us, probably holding a gun to poor Snoop's head—I really don't know why he chose that name because he was hella fine with a long dick. He looked waaaaay better than Snoop Dogg. Anyway, Big South and Nolan thought we were all having dinner together or something like that. I didn't even tell Neil the truth for fear of him telling his crazy-ass brothers, but to be honest, as fun as this party full of my freaky friends and family was, this dude didn't have shit on Neil. Neil was just...*it*. And now that we'd decided to have sex after we got married, he was virtually the only thing on my mind most waking hours of the day. Right at that moment, while Snoop Dong shook his ass in my face, I was visualizing what Neil's naked ass looked like and recalling how big his hands were, the muscles in his arms, that damn six pack that taunted me when he was shirtless around me, the way he smelled, his smile, his eyes, his lips and how they felt when he practice-kissed me, how his mouth tasted—

Snoop Dong grabbed my hand, pulled me to my feet, and lifted me up, wrapping my legs around his waist, and as he went about the business of air-screwing me, I closed my eyes and imagined he was my fiancé.

Neil

Three days before the wedding...

She dropped it low and put her hands on her knees as she twerked her ass to the music. I adjusted in my seat as I watched her booty bounce like it had a damn motor in it while Blac Youngster's *Booty* filled the club.

Her ass jiggled up and down and then she spread her legs, sliding into a split, and started bouncing to the music again. Damn, this chick had talent.

And a big ass.

But the crazy thing was, the whole time this stripper — I think her name was Juicy — performed, it made me think of Sage. I'd seen her dance before. Shit, she could twerk just as good as this chick if my memory was correct. Then I started wondering what Sage's naked body looked like. I'd seen those thick thighs and legs. *I bet her naked ass will make a grown man cry.*

I shook my head a little, told myself to stop thinking about shit like that before I ended up with a hard dick I couldn't do anything about. Because I was not screwing that stripper. I was saving myself for my wife.

The fuck was I saying?

My eyes toured the club — *Second Avenue*. No one was drinking, thanks to a very considerate Everett, so things weren't too wild. Hell, my three brothers had their faces in their phones. Wasn't no one going to catch them with their eyes on Juicy *or* her remarkable ass. They were trying to maintain their happy homes. I was trying to build one, I think. Well, I was trying to do *something* with Sage, and on my mama, the shit felt right. Her living in my house? Me marrying her? Us planning to fuck? All of that felt like a natural progression, an accelerated version of what was supposed to happen in a romantic relationship. The shit didn't make sense, so I mostly kept my feelings to myself until my counseling sessions, which had been more frequent as of late. Mother Erica knew it all.

"Peace, power, and light, my brother."

I looked up to see Jeremy Unger, one of the first friends I made when I moved to LA. I hadn't talked to dude in years, partially because of being messed up in the head for so long, and also because Jeremy could be on some bullshit sometimes. Nolan had made the guest list for this bachelor party. How the hell did he get in touch with this dude?

"Peace, power, and light," I responded.

"How you feeling, man? You ready for this? Ready to get hitched, jump the broom?"

"Yeah, man," I answered. "I'm ready."

He fell into the chair next to mine, his eyes glued to Juicy's booty. "Well, congrats, man. Good to see you got your shit together. And I hear your fiancée is a baddie. One of them thick ones."

I didn't like the way he said that shit and had to wonder who was saying stuff like that about Sage. "Where you hear that?" I asked.

"Well, actually...I saw some pics Big South's wife posted of her on IG. She's a winner, man!"

"Yeah...thanks, man. She's a catch, for sure. I'm a lucky man."

"Yeah, yeah...where you meet her? Through South's wife?"

I eyed him. What was this nigga on? Probably some bullshit, like I said. "Yeah," I replied.

"That's cool, man. Y'all keeping it all in the family and shit, huh?"

"Uh-huh."

"Can't wait to meet her at the wedding."

He left, and I followed him with my eyes. I hoped I wouldn't have to put my foot up Jeremy's shifty ass over Sage. *Wait, where did that come from?*

"What that nigga want? I don't trust his ass. He always looking shifty and shit," Leland said, taking the seat Jeremy vacated.

"I know. I don't know why Nolan invited him, but then again, I don't fuck with a lot of people, so the options were few."

"What he want?"

"Asking about Sage. He better not be on no shit with her, though."

When I turned to look at my little brother, my only little brother since Nolan was a few minutes older than me, he was staring at me with a frown.

Finally, he leaned in close to me, and whispered, "I thought this was a fake marriage."

"Fake or not, I don't want that motherfucker messing with her. She's still gonna be my wife!"

"My bad, nigga. Shit. So...you really are good with marrying her, huh?"

"I'm better than good with it," I said, standing from my seat. I was over Juicy's show and being surrounded by folks I'd lost touch with long ago. Most of them were from the conscious community but were sleep as a motherfucker. But shit, I used to be the same way; that's why I associated with them back in the day. Now I knew better. Anyway, I would've been cool with just a little get-together with my brothers.

I walked out into the club's lobby and pulled out my phone to text Sage.

Me: *What you doing?*

Sage: *Eating up all your dried apricots. They are good as hell!*

Me: *That's fucked up.*

Sage: *Whatever. What you doing? Being nasty at that party? Y'all got strippers and shit?*

Me: *Currently? I'm texting you, missing you.*

Sage: *Don't say stuff like that if you don't mean it.*

Me: *I mean it.*

Sage: *In that case, I miss you too. Hurry home so you can burn your incense and meditate and read your books.*

I chuckled as I typed out: *I was thinking it's time for me to burn some sage. You ready for me to set you on fire?*

Sage: *There you go talking that shit again.*

Me: *And I can't wait to back it up.*

10

Sage

Two days before the wedding...

"What did you say we're doing? Explain this shit again, please," Jo said, taking the words from my mind.

"We are going in there to get a yoni steam treatment. Think of it as a pussy facial. I hear it's life-changing."

"So you've never done this before? Hooker, I'm not going in there letting them steam the skin off my thing-thing!" I shouted.

"Aww, yeah! There she is! Good to have you back, friend," Bridgette yelled, raising her hand for a high-five from me.

"I ain't high-fiving your crazy ass! Why are we doing this, anyway? I mean, I get why we did the mani, pedi, facial, eyebrow threading, my braids—" I swung my head from side to side. "That's all wedding prep, but a coochie facial? Girl, please."

"I'm with Sage, Bridge. I'm not feeling this at all," Jo said.

"But it's good for you!" Bridgette declared.

"How the hell do you know if you've never done it before?" I asked.

"Because I did the damn research. Hell, I ain't tryna mess my own pussy up when I got that good got-damn *Gone with the Wind* dick at home. Shit!"

I rolled my eyes while at the same time wondering if good dick was something twins had in common. "Fine. What are the damn benefits, then?"

"Okay, you bitches listen," Bridgette said.

Jo sighed loudly. "Heifer, would you come on with this? We are three black women sitting in a damn spa parking lot in America. Some white woman be done called the cops on us for existing."

"I'm trying to. Damn!"

"Got-damn, Bridge! Tell us!" I said.

"If you two don't shut the hell up! Anyway, it helps reduce stress, boosts energy, it's supposed to be really relaxing, and it makes your punani wetter."

"Aw, shit...I'm in, then. The wetter my coochie is, the better," Jo said.

Then they both looked at me perched in the backseat, and Bridgette asked, "What about you, Sage?"

I shrugged and twisted my mouth to the side. "I guess I'm in. I don't suppose it'll hurt anything."

"Good! Let's go," Bridgette chirped, hopping out of her car.

"Shit, the wetter my pussy is, the better, too," I mumbled, as I climbed out of the car.

"You say something, Sage?" Jo asked.

I shook my head. "Nope."

"Wait," Bridgette said, once we made it to the front door.

"Aw, hell...what?" Jo asked.

"Y'all not on your periods, are you?"

"No," Jo and I said in unison.

"Anybody pregnant?" Bridgette asked.

"Hell no!" Jo and I said in unison again.

"Do either of you still have IUDs?"

"You know I got mine removed so I could conceive Lena. I'm on the pill, now," Jo said.

"And you know I ain't never had an IUD. I'm too scared to get one," I reminded her.

Bridgette released a sigh. "Good, because you're not supposed to do this if you have an IUD or are pregnant or on your period."

"What about you? You got an IUD," Jo pointed out.

"Not anymore."

"Oh, shit! Y'all tryna have a baby?!" I screamed.

"Shit, no! I still ain't having no babies. Y'all gotta leave that alone. Having babies is not every woman's dream."

"I know that, but why you take the IUD out, then?" I asked.

"I just decided to switch it up. I got the patch now," Bridgette explained.

"Oh," Jo and I chorused.

A few minutes later, we were inside of the Amani Day Spa, in individual dressing rooms. I quickly peeled off my leggings and long t-shirt and pulled on the gown dress thing the lady who greeted us provided. After I had the strapless, gold-embossed dress on, I inspected myself in the mirror, took in my thick body, my meaty shoulders, my full face, my lips and nose, ran my fingers through my tiny braids, and sighed. Closing my eyes, I hoped I was doing the right thing and that somehow this marriage wouldn't end up being a clusterfuck. Shit, I didn't want to somehow drive the man to drink again. I liked Sober Neil.

I dug my phone out of my purse to shut it off so that I could "foster the peace of the ritual," as our hostess put it, and a text came through almost the second I touched the phone.

Neil: *I was just sitting here listening to some Gil Scott-Heron and thinking about how many orgasms I'ma give you on our wedding night.*

With a grin on my face, I replied: *Gil Scott-Heron makes you horny?*

Neil: *Your young ass knows who he was?*

Me: *I'm not that damn young, Neil. I'm almost thirty, only like seven or eight years younger than you.*

Neil: *You young as hell, baby.*

Baby? Damn, that made my clit jump.

Me: *Whatever.*

Neil: *Anyway, I was thinking about giving you orgasms before I started listening to him. I started listening to him to take my mind off you. Didn't work. I'm sitting here hard as hell right now.*

I had to sit down on the little bench in the dressing area and fan myself. Shoot, my yoni was *already* steaming.

Me: *Neil?*

Neil: *Yeah, baby?*

Shit!

Me: *I gotta go.*

Neil: *Okay. I'ma go take a damn cold shower.*

I giggled and responded with: *Have fun.*

All three of us sat on individual custom-built wooden boxes on platforms. They were kind of like wooden toilets, but instead of us sitting over a bowl of toilet water, the hostess placed a steaming hot ceramic bowl of water and herbs in the box, instructing us to sit over the hole like we would a toilet bowl. Then she helped us drape our gowns around us to trap the steam underneath.

It felt like...shit, I can't even describe it. It was so warm, like there was a gentle heat lamp trained on my yoni, and I felt all these sensations down there that made me close my eyes and just bask in the peace of that place. The music piped into the room was so calming, and the steaming ritual was so cleansing, that when the twenty or so minutes had passed and our hostess came to retrieve us, I didn't want to move a muscle. I didn't want to leave. I don't think Bridgette or Jo did either.

Once we'd gotten dressed and climbed into Bridgette's car to leave, we were all quiet, still vibrating from the experience until Bridgette announced, "I feel like I got a new pussy. I mean, it's like I got my teenage pussy back. Shit, I can't wait to do that again!"

"Girl, me either! That was sooo good!" I yelled.

"Hell, I'ma figure out how to do that shit at home!" Jo informed us.

We went on and on about how good it felt and how much we loved it. Jo even did an Internet search on her phone and found a site that sold the yoni-steaming herbs and custom-made seats. But while we discussed the experience, what I didn't share was how horny it'd made me feel. I was so got-damn hot, I wasn't sure me and Neil were gonna make it to the honeymoon before I attacked his fine ass.

But unfortunately, he wasn't home when I made it there.

Neil

It was late when I made it home. I'd decided to spend some time at my bookstore, had a meeting with my manager, and looked over the store's sales stats. I couldn't do nothing but be thankful it was still doing so well seeing as my ass had been too busy fucking my life up to give it any attention. Anyway, I ended up helping out with running the register, talked to some of the regular patrons, ordered some books, had lunch with Nolan on the same block as the bookstore, and then sent my manager home and took care of some paperwork. I grabbed a couple of Buddha bowls from one of my favorite restaurants for me and Sage's dinner and was happy to see her car in my driveway when I pulled up.

The house was dark, quiet when I stepped inside, and I figured she'd knocked out early because Bridgette and Jo had been running the shit out of her that week. I walked into the dark kitchen, and when I heard, "You finally made it home, huh?" I damn near dropped our food.

Flicking the light on, I turned to see her sitting at the kitchen table wearing a short t-shirt and a pair of those booty shorts she liked to sleep in. I swallowed and nodded. "Yeah…got caught up at my store. Had some work to catch up on."

"Oh."

"What you doing sitting here in the dark?"

"Thinking."

"About what?"

"I was wondering if we could practice on that kiss again?"

I set the food down. "Uh, yeah…sure."

She stood from the chair, her breasts bouncing in that little-ass shirt as she walked toward me, then she wrapped her arms around my neck, and said, "With tongue."

Before I could agree, because I was definitely going to agree, her mouth was on me and her tongue was bumping against mine. I squeezed her to me, tilted my head to the side, and deepened the kiss. When she cocked her leg up around my waist, I grabbed her ass and helped her wrap her other leg around me. Then she started grinding on me, making my damn dick jump to attention. I stumbled back against the counter, gripping her ass like I'd fall if I let it go. She kept grinding on me, moaning into my mouth as we kissed, and all kinds of nasty, crazy shit was running through my mind.

She moved faster and faster against me, kissed me harder, and I felt like I was floating outside my body. It'd been years since I felt anything like this, since I'd had a woman in my arms, and it felt like pure Heaven. And the sight of her being lost in the moment, losing control like that? That shit was everything.

I felt her stiffen, and as she threw her head back with her mouth open, I sucked on her neck while squeezing her ass tightly. And I'll be damned if I didn't bust right there, clothes on and everything. That nut was so powerful, I almost dropped her. Then the air in the kitchen was filled with our lurid breathing as we both came down from a high only a good orgasm could induce.

"I-I brought dinner," I finally said, as I rested my forehead against hers, still trying to catch my breath.

She shook her head. "I can't eat. Too damn exhausted now."

"Shit, me too."

I placed her on the floor, and before she could turn to leave the kitchen, I said, "Sage?"

"Yeah?" she responded, eyes wide with an innocence that was nowhere to be found moments earlier.

"Good night."

She smiled up at me and blinked her eyes drowsily. "Good night, Neil."

11

Neil

One day before the wedding...

"...yeah. Saturday...thanks! No, I'm not working next week either. I'll be on my honeymoon. Uh-huh. Sure! Okay, I'll hit you up then." Sage ended her call and blew out a breath.

"Damn," I said, "your customers stay blowing up your phone, don't they?"

She rolled over on her side on my sofa. "Yeah. They been tripping about me not working this week or next week, But I'm like, shit! I'm getting married, y'all. A couple of these fools actually tryna pay me to do their makeup for my own wedding! Where the hell they do that at?!"

I chuckled. "Yeah, that's fucked up."

She flipped back to her stomach and was about to put those earbuds back in her ears and stare at that laptop again, when I said, "What you be looking at on that computer all the time?"

She pursed her lips. "Well, since you ain't got a TV, this is my only source of entertainment."

"That doesn't tell me what you're looking at."

"If you must know, I'm looking at 4C Angie on YouTube."

"Who?"

"She's a natural hair vlogger."

I lifted my eyebrows and stared at her.

She sat up on the couch and patted the cushion beside her. "Come here, and I'll show you."

I moved from my recliner and sat beside her, my eyes on the computer screen.

"See, she does videos about natural hair care, and she does stuff with her husband and their little boy, too. Recently, she's started doing makeup reviews, so that's what I'm watching now."

"Damn, she got a lotta hair!"

"I know! My shit will never grow like that. I tried."

"I like your cut, but how the hell they attach braids to hair that short?" I asked.

"My girl, Hera, be working miracles. Bridgette was tryna take me to this expensive-ass salon, and I was like shiiidd, you better take me to Hera's crib where I can get a fly hairdo and watch all the latest movies on bootleg at the same damn time!"

I laughed. "You a trip, but I'm glad your ass loosened up around me. Stopped acting all shy and shit."

She dropped her eyes. "I had to adjust. But you helped with that, being nice to me and all."

"And making you come?"

"I actually made myself come. I just used you to get it done."

"Word?"

"Mm-hmm."

"Okay, if you say so…"

She lifted her eyes and licked her lips, and I had to close my eyes for a second. "What you be reading all the time? Every time I see you, you're in a different book. You ever finish one?" she asked.

"I always finish a book before starting another one. I just read fast."

"So, all them books I've seen you reading? You finished them?"

"Yeah."

"I've been here, what, a week, right?"

"No, baby…nine days."

Her eyes flashed, and she cleared her throat. "Yeah…so

how many books have you read since I've been staying here?"

I thought about her question, and said, "Seven, I think."

"Damn! You really like reading, huh?"

"I like gaining knowledge. Knowledge is power. That's why the oppressors tried to keep us from reading, so reading is also an act of rebellion, and I'm nothing if not a rebel. You don't read?"

"Naw. I mean, I used to. Back in the day, I loved any book with the word 'thug' in the title."

"Damn, for real?"

"Yep."

"Why'd you stop reading them?"

"Because I started messing with thugs in real life."

"You like rough necks, huh?"

"I used to."

"Your last man was a thug?"

"A fake one."

"Hmm."

"What were you reading before I called you over here?"

I glanced over at the book I'd left sitting in the recliner. "*The Fire This Time*, a book of poetry and essays about race."

"Sounds too heavy for me. Is everything you read that serious? You ever read fun stuff?"

"That's fun to me."

"If you say so..."

I smiled. "Well, I'll let you get back to YouTube. You're spending the night with Jo and Ev after the rehearsal dinner, right?"

"Yep."

"You riding to the rehearsal with me?"

"Uh-huh. Unless you don't want me to."

"Why wouldn't I want you to?"

"I'm just saying."

"Naw, you're just tripping."

"You know, this'll be the last night you'll get to spend in this house without me..."

"And my last night without you in my bed."

"You want me to move into your bedroom after the honeymoon?"

"Baby, after I put this Superdick on you, your ass is gonna *want* to move into my bedroom."

"There you go with that shit again."

"You'll see."

"...I guess those of you who don't know me have figured out Neil is my twin. I'm the oldest but Neil is the smartest, always has been. And he's got a bigger heart, which makes it easy for him to get hurt."

"Damn, Nole. You got me sounding like a simp, man," I mumbled, making the people gathered around Everett's huge dining room table laugh.

"Naw, it's nothing but love, man," Nolan said.

"Nole, can you wrap it up? We ain't tryna be here when it's time for the wedding," Everett quipped.

More laughs.

"Man, I ain't even that long-winded," Nolan said.

"Yes, you are," Bridgette countered.

I chuckled.

Nolan shook his head. "It be your own people. Anyway, I just want to wish my twin and Sage the best." He lifted his glass, and the rest of us followed suit.

After Nolan took his seat, I draped my arm over the back of Sage's chair and rubbed her shoulder, leaned into her ear, and softly said, "I'ma tear your ass up when we get to Palm Springs."

She whispered, "You better have me damn near crippled, or I'm kicking your fine ass."

I threw my head back and laughed.

"Can I have everybody's attention?" Sage's father said, as

he stood from his chair, glass in hand. I couldn't help but notice his Liberian accent was weak as hell. Sage had said he was laying it on for me before, and now I believed her. I glanced over at her as she lifted her eyebrows, and mouthed, "I told you."

I shook my head with a grin on my face and returned my attention to her father.

"There's a saying in Liberia that goes like this: 'Let your love be like the misty rain, coming softly, but flooding the river.' Sage, Neil, your love came quick, so quick I wasn't sure it was real. But looking at you two now, seeing how happy you look together, how you look at my daughter, Neil, I can feel the love. So all you two need to do now, is to keep building on that love, little by little like a trickling misty rain, and your rivers will always overflow with affection for each other. Sage, I'm proud of you, and I wish you both a lifetime of happiness." Then he lifted his glass, and I heard sniffing to my left.

"You okay, baby?" I asked, kissing her cheek.

She nodded. "Yeah, I'm okay. I just...I hate lying to everyone."

"What did I say about this marriage thing? We can make it real. And shit, it doesn't feel like a lie to me. Not anymore."

She wiped her eyes and gave me a frail smile. "Thank you again for doing this, Neil," Her voice was almost indiscernible.

"Maybe I should be thanking you. You've given my miserable ass a reason to smile again."

"Really?"

"Really."

"Can I hug you?"

I wrapped my arms around her and let her cry into my chest, and as I closed my eyes and held her to me, the entire table sang, "Awwwww."

12

Sage

The wedding day...

"I told you to let me pay someone to do your makeup! You shaking and shit, got lipstick all over your damn nose!" Bridgette fussed, as she yanked a tissue from a box and swiped at my nose.

"That ain't gonna get it off. This lipstick is fucking bulletproof! Shit! What is wrong with my hands?!" I screamed, throwing the tube of burnt sienna lipstick on the vanity.

"Sage, sweetie, I know this is nerve-wracking. Remember how jacked up I was before my wedding? Shit, I swore I was gonna walk down the aisle and Everett wouldn't be waiting for me. I was soooo anxious," Jo said.

"Your situation was different, and you know it!" I covered my face with my hands, propping my elbows on the vanity.

"Hey, can y'all give us a minute alone with her?" I heard Bridgette say.

"Why? She's my damn sister!"

"And my cousin!"

I popped my head up. "Ferula, Audrina, go!"

"Damn, okay," my sister muttered.

Bridgette closed the door behind them and stomped over to me in her gorgeous co-matron of honor dress.

"You look so pretty, Bridge," I whimpered.

"Thank you. Sage, sweetie…do you want to do this? If you don't, we'll understand. I know you want to stay in the states, but marrying a man you don't really know is a big thing. Maybe you could try with Gavin again?" Bridgette said softly.

"Yeah, don't worry about the money spent or anything. We just want you to be okay. You don't have to marry Neil," Jo soothed.

I wiped my wet eyes and took a deep breath. "Can I be alone for a few minutes?"

"Yeah," Bridgette and Jo said at the same time. After they both hugged me, they left, and I picked up my phone from the chair beside me, looked around the hotel room, then peered into my portable lighted mirror at myself.

After I dialed the number, I closed my eyes and took a deep breath.

"You backing out on me?"

I smiled despite the turmoil filling my mind. Neil's voice sounded so good to me. Shit, it always had. "I'm a wreck. I'm so scared."

"Hold on," he said, then I heard him asking who I assumed were his brothers to give him a minute. "All right, I'm back. What you scared of?"

I opened my eyes and looked at myself in the mirror again. "Falling in love with you. What do I do if that happens?"

"Let me love you back."

"But…I don't have the best track record with love. My expectations are low."

"Then let me free you of those expectations, give you what *I* have to give."

"But you don't know me…not really."

"I wanna know you. *Let me* know you."

"Damn, you talk a good game."

"It ain't game, Sage. Can I be real with you for a moment?"
"Yeah."

"Okay…at first, I didn't want to do this. When Ev and Nole approached me about it, I thought they were out of their minds, but now? I want to marry you more than I've ever wanted anything in my life. If you don't marry me, I will be devastated."

"Why? Because you wanna fuck me?"

"I gotta marry you to fuck you?"

Hell no. "You got a point there."

He chuckled into the phone. "Look, don't be nervous or anxious or scared. One thing I strongly believe in is destiny. This is our destiny. You're supposed to be my wife, okay? And I can't wait to call you Mrs. Neil McClain."

"Neil?"

"Yeah, baby?"

"I'll see you at the altar. I need to finish getting ready."

"I'll be waiting for you."

Neil

She was beautiful, her eyes on me through that veil as her father escorted her down the aisle in the grand ballroom at the Sable-Beverly Hills Hotel. As she floated toward me, I felt my chest tighten and my pants tighten and a smile creep across my face. All those months ago, when I was sneaking liquor into Everett's house and betting on stupid-ass ball games and shit, I never thought I'd be standing there in that fly-ass tuxedo, about to marry my rib.

My wife.

The woman the Creator made for me was about to be *my wife.*

As she and her father inched down the aisle, my mind drifted back to that day in Mother Erica's office and what she told me after I charged in there ranting about how stupid

Everett and Nolan were for asking me to marry a woman I barely knew.

"Neil," *she said in that voice of hers that she never raised.* "Sit down, son."

I did without hesitation because of the word son. She knew that got to me, too. She was fighting dirty.

"She's from The Continent? Liberia, you say?"

"Yes."

"Her name?"

"What?"

"What is her name, Neil?"

"Sage...Sage Moniba."

She grew quiet, leaning back with her eyes closed, a posture she usually took when she wanted to hear from the ancestors. Then she opened her eyes and fixed them on me. "Marry her."

"What?! No disrespect, but hell naw!"

"Neil, it is no accident that she needs a husband and you are available to be one. It is no accident that you have undergone this transformation at this time when she needs your help. She is the reason my spirit urged me to release you. She is also the reason you felt you weren't ready."

"Huh? What does that mean?"

"What do we use sage for? The herb."

I shrugged. "Uh, it has medicinal purposes. And if you burn it, it clears the atmosphere of negativity. It —"

"It heals. It purifies and brings peace to spaces. It's sacred in its usefulness. And so is she. She's the last piece of your journey to wholeness. Marry her."

"I don't understand."

"It's not for you to understand. You don't have to understand to be obedient. Did you understand all the things your mother instructed you to do when you were a child?"

"Not initially, but she made me understand by explaining herself to me."

"So did I. She's your peace, your healing, your soul mate. Marry her, Neil. Once you marry her, you'll understand."

When I left her office, I was confused and conflicted, but after a night of dreams that shook my soul, I was certain that Mother Erica was right. Sage was my wife, my future.

And now, there I was, taking her hand as her father presented her to me, seeing the anxious look in her eyes. I lifted her veil, took in her beauty — almond-shaped eyes, strong nose, enticing lips, skin the color of dark syrup and just as smooth, tiny braids in curls around her pretty face — and leaned in close to her ear. "You look stunning, baby. I can't wait to lick the crack of your ass tonight," I whispered.

Her eyes widened as she turned and faced the preacher, giving him a nervous smile.

"Dearly beloved, we are gathered here today to join this king and this queen in holy matrimony…"

I focused on the preacher as he began the ceremony, and when Sage reached for my hand, I grabbed hers and squeezed it.

He was so handsome standing there waiting for me with his best men — Big South, Leland, and Nolan — by his side. Nolan was on his immediate left. Now that was a mind fuck. Two identical men in suits watching me walk down the aisle. But besides the differences in their suits — both were white, but Nolan's tie was black — I knew which one was Neil because of the look in his eyes as he stared at me and the smile on his face that was now familiar to me. When he smiled like that, it felt like it was a smile especially reserved for me. That didn't make sense, but it felt so real to me that I believed it to be true, just like I believed him when he said he'd be devastated if I didn't marry him.

To the left of the altar stood my matrons of honor—Jo, Bridgette, and my sister—all looking gorgeous in their white dresses. Side note, my mother made me make my sister a matron of honor. Otherwise, that wouldn't have happened. But anyway, they looked good, and the smiles on my friends' faces warmed my heart.

I felt giddy by the time my father presented me to Neil, and when he whispered that nasty shit in my ear after he lifted my veil, my stomach flip-flopped and my clit jumped. He was so wrong for that.

The ceremony was beautiful, infused with Neil's hotep request of us being referred to as king and queen right down to the preacher's declaration of, "I now pronounce you husband and wife. King Neil, you may kiss your queen."

And then, that five-foot-eleven, one hundred and ninety pound, fine-ass man pulled me into his arms and kissed me like he'd lost his last dollar in my mouth and desperately needed to find it. As our family and friends cheered around us, I got lost in that kiss, wrapping my arms around him. And when he finally released me, he cupped my face in his hands, smiled down at me, and said, "Thank you."

My only thought was, *He's thanking me?* But my response was to pull his mouth back to mine, and all around us, I could hear whistles and more cheers.

13

Neil

We entered the room where the reception was held to upbeat Liberian music, some song Sage said was about love and marriage. She danced into the room in front of me in a long purple and gold dress that fit her ass just right, and with that ass as my motivation, I danced right behind her in my matching outfit. Her aunts and mom laid down these fabrics for us to step on, and they, along with other members of her family, surrounded us once we were in the middle of the room and threw money at us and cheered us on.

I was grinning like a fool as I stared at Sage's ass and tried to concentrate on dancing as she bent over at the waist and moved her shoulders to the music. When she turned to face me, she was smiling bigger than I'd ever seen her smile before. She raised her arms as she danced closer to me, and I grabbed her, moving to the music as I kissed her while money rained down on us. The music, seeing all her relatives in their Liberian garb? Damn, it all felt so good, like this was meant to be. I guess that's because it was.

It really was.

"...welcome to our family, Neil!" One of Sage's uncles finally ended his speech, and everyone raised their glasses. There was wine available to the guests, but I was drinking water and I was cool with it. Shit, I was on cloud nine. I didn't need to be inebriated.

We sat at the head table, my hand on her thigh, as tons of people stood from their seats and toasted us, including Nolan's long-winded ass. Damn, Sage had a big-ass family. A lot of them had flown in from the east coast for the wedding, but a few lived in Cali. Her sister had traveled from Canada where she lived with her Canadian husband. I wondered how many of Sage's family members Forty-five was kicking out of the country, then wiped that thought out of my mind. I didn't want to be angry on my wedding day. Anger and guilt were what fucked me up before.

"Uh, for those of you who don't know me, I'm Lee Chester Amerson—Neil's Uncle—"

"What up. Unc?!" Everett shouted from his seat, interrupting Uncle Lee Chester.

"What-up-there-now, Nephew?! Uh, like I was saying, Neil's mama, Juanita Jean, was my sister, God rest her soul, and I just wanted to congratulate my nephew on getting married. You know, this boy always been real smart, so it don't surprise me none that he married a librarian. He always did love him some books."

"Shit," I mumbled. Why me?

Sage smacked her hand over her mouth, trying to keep from laughing.

I watched as Leland stood from his seat and whispered in Uncle Lee's ear. As Leland reclaimed his seat, Uncle Lee said, "Shit, that explains it! She from Africa. I ain't know what the hell was going on with the music and the African clothes. I just figured all that had to do with some black power stuff since Neil is into that...anyway, I just wanna say, Juanita Jean would be proud of her kids. Especially you, Neil. Wish my Lou was here to see this, but her ass won't step over the damn threshold of our trailer for nothing but Thursday night bingo. Anyhow, I'm glad you straightened yourself out and got you a nice African wife, Neil. I know that's a dream come true for you. Boy, you gonna have fuuuuun tonight with that jungle boogie! Gon' get you some wild cat! Cheers, y'all!"

Sage's mother and fifty-eleven aunts all gasped.

I dropped my head and shook it.

"OMG, I love him!" Sage gushed beside me.

Sage

My feet hurt from all the dancing, but I didn't care. This all felt so good! And I can't lie, it felt great to know my future in the states was no longer hanging in the balance.

Neil pulled me to him and started grinding on me to J-Max's *Marry You*. The DJ had been playing a nice mix of R&B and Liberian music, mostly upbeat like this one, and Neil somehow managed to find a way to grind to all of it. He was nasty as hell.

And I loved it.

I turned around and rolled my booty on him, hoping my parents couldn't see us as he grabbed my hips and held my butt against his erection. Spinning around with wide eyes, I watched him nod and mouth, "It's going down tonight."

I laughed as he grabbed me and kissed my neck.

"I don't know what you laughing at," he said into my ear. "I'm about to shoot the club up!"

I backed away from him a bit, and replied, "You better."

The song had ended, and we were heading back to our seats when a familiar voice blared from the speakers.

"I requested this next song special for Neil and Sadie. Y'all get back out there and dance to it!" Uncle Lee Chester announced.

"Shit, I know this is gonna be bad," Neil muttered, as he took my hand and led me back to the dancefloor.

"Maybe not," I said, trying not to laugh at Neil's distress.

"And what the fuck does he have on?" Neil asked.

I really had to fight not to bust out laughing at that, because his uncle was looking a whole mess in that tight-ass, circa 1982 suit he had on.

"Here we go!" Uncle Lee Chester shouted, and then the music started. *Liberian Girl* by Michael Jackson.

"Goooot damn," Neil said, shaking his head.

"Wow," was my response.

"I am so damn shame right now. Who the fuck invited Uncle Lee?" Neil murmured.

"Y'all ain't dancing!" Nolan shouted.

"I'ma kick Nolan's ass. I promise I am," Neil said.

"Yeah, get on out there, Nephew! Want me to show you how to do it?!" Uncle Lee Chester yelled in the microphone, and before Neil could reply, the older man was out on the dancefloor slipping and sliding in his shiny black church shoes, his white socks easily visible in his too-short slacks.

"If he keeps on, he's gonna bust the ass of those booty-cutters he got on," Neil muttered.

I giggled, but I could not take my eyes off of his uncle.

"Come on, baby. Let's dance before Uncle Lee requests *Africa* by Toto or some shit," Neil said.

"What's that?" I asked.

"Young ass…"

14

Sage

The honeymoon...

He was quiet on the drive to Palm Springs. At first, I thought maybe he was concentrating on the road; then I realized his energy seemed lower than what I'd grown accustomed to, and like I was prone to doing, I started overthinking. As I sat in the passenger seat of his Tahoe, I decided he was having second thoughts, regretting marrying me, and probably sitting behind that steering wheel trying to decide how to break it to me that he wanted an annulment. Shit, I wasn't even sure what an annulment was, but I knew it was something people who hadn't been married long got.

What if he doesn't want an annulment but just doesn't want to fuck me anymore? I was really looking forward to that, because Jo and Bridgette have been getting it good. Good sex runs in families, right? I knew he was going to keep talking that big shit and not back it up.

I sighed, fixing my eyes on the windshield, then chanced a quick glance at my new husband, who was probably about to be my ex-husband. His eyes were on the road, his forehead creased in concentration.

Shit, he's fine! Got those big-ass hands. Lord! Wait, what if he's not thinking about leaving me, but he's worried because he's got a little pee-pee?

Naw, bitch. You know you felt a monster when you were dry-humping him.

Oh, yeah...that's right.

I was actually having an internal back-and-forth conversation with myself. What the fuck?

I dug in my purse and pulled out my phone, quickly finding myself smiling at all the pictures my family and friends had posted from the wedding. There was one of Neil and I dancing during our reception entrance with money raining down on us. We were both wearing the biggest smiles.

As I reposted it, I thought about something. "Hey, what's your IG name?"

"My what?" he asked, eyes still on the road.

"Your IG name. I wanna tag you in this picture of us."

"Oh...I don't do social media anymore, baby."

There he went calling me baby again. Maybe all was not lost...

"You don't? You don't even have Facebook? All the old people have Facebook."

That got him to smile. "You got jokes, huh? We gonna see how old this dick is when we get to this hotel."

That made *me* smile, and we spent the rest of the almost two-hour drive talking shit to each other.

"This is nice. I didn't know there was a Sable Inns Resort here, but I'm glad we're staying in a black-owned establishment," Neil shared.

I nodded, eying the huge bed. "Yeah..."

"You tired? Wanna lay down for a while, take a nap? It's been a long day," he asked, as I took in the rest of the beautiful suite.

"No, I'm good. I'm not really that tired at all," I replied.

"Really?"

"Yeah, but I need to take a shower. I'm feeling grimy after all that dancing."

He plopped down on the bed and fell onto his back. "All right. I'ma take one after you."

In the huge, glass-enclosed shower, as I closed my eyes and let the hot water beat against my skin, I told myself that whenever this sex thing went down, if it wasn't good, I'd be okay with it. I mean, sex wasn't everything, and if he didn't annul my ass, he'd done me a huge favor. Shit, he didn't really know me like that to be marrying me. I mean, after all the pussy, time, and effort I'd put into my past relationships, none of those niggas had met me at the altar.

Assholes.

The chief asshole was Gavin. This motherfucker had said some horrible stuff to me when I asked him to marry me, some stuff that really messed with my head and had me feeling like I was sub-human. And when I cried about it, he—

First I felt a draft; then I felt the heat of his body and my eyes popped open. Spinning around, my eyes widened, and I stuttered, "W-what—Neil?" I don't know why I said that. Maybe his fine-ness was messing with my brain, because he was naked and good Lord! This man was fine as all hell and Heaven and everywhere in between!

"Were you expecting someone else?"

"N-no...I thought you were gonna take a shower when I was done."

"I ain't in here to take a shower." My eyes dropped to watch him stroke his nice, long, veiny dick, then shot back up to his face as he said, "I'm in here to fuck my sexy-ass wife."

My yoni started throbbing as if it was dancing to a high-octane club banger, and my hands began to shake, moisture collected in my mouth like I was a lion staring at a gazelle in the Serengeti, and through no will of my own, I grabbed his face and pulled it down to mine, kissing him with the fervor of a woman who'd never seen an exposed, erect penis before.

He backed me up under the shower head into the wall, and

despite the fact that I knew without a doubt I was messing up my hair, I didn't stop him. We kissed wildly, passionately. No, passionately is too weak a word, because this nigga actually bit my tongue, and my lip, and he was growling while squeezing my breasts, and I liked all of it.

Hell, I *loved* it.

He ended the kiss, and as my chest rose and fell rapidly, he planted one hand on the shower wall beside my head while using the fingers of the other hand to explore my yoni, parting my lips to find my clit. He rubbed it, holding my eyes hostage and biting his bottom lip as he slid a finger inside me, making my knees buckle. Then he kissed me again, slipping his finger in and out of me while circling my clit with his thumb, gradually increasing the speed of his fingers until it felt frenzied. There was more than one finger inside me now — two? Three? And he was touching a spot that felt different, some uncharted territory inside me that made me feel good and uncomfortable at the same time. Hella uncomfortable and hella good. He had me feeling like I had to pee and come simultaneously. It was confusing in a wonderful way.

"Oh! Ohhhhhh, shhhit!" I yelled into his mouth.

My entire body vibrated with a feeling that was alien to me. It was like I was having a damn global orgasm. My scalp was tingling, it felt like heat was enveloping me, and electricity shot through my body as I shuddered uncontrollably. He grabbed me with his free hand to keep me from falling, as the other hand continued to assault me.

"Yeah, baby…feel it," he kept saying, his deep voice coarse. "Feel it."

What the fuck was this? I mean, it'd never been hard for me to orgasm, but this shit? This was beyond an orgasm. This was…this was *spiritual*. And it went on, and on, and on.

When my body finally came down, I collapsed into his arms, and I swear on everything, I think I passed out.

*****

I woke up naked and in the dark, lying alone in the bed. At first, I lay there staring at the ceiling, then felt eyes on me and turned to my left. "Neil?" I couldn't see him, but I was sure he was there.

"I'm here, baby."

I felt my body relax at that reassurance. "How long have I been asleep?"

"A couple of hours."

"Damn."

"A g-spot orgasm will do that to you. That, plus the long-ass day we had."

"That's what that was? I thought that was coochie hoodoo or something. I could've sworn you put a sex hex on me."

He laughed. "Naw, baby. You never had an orgasm like that before?"

"No. Never. That was...that was crazy. Good, but crazy. Did you...did you get off, too?"

"No."

"Oh. You didn't want to?"

"You blacked out. I'm not in the business of having sex with unconscious women."

"That makes sense. So...you've just been sitting there while I sleep?"

"Uh-huh."

"Okay..."

"Sage?"

"Yeah?"

"I'd like to eat your pussy."

Shit! "You would?"

"Yeah, I wanna taste you."

Dayum! "Uh, knock yourself out. I ain't gonna stop you."

With a chuckle, he left the chair, and in the darkness, I felt him pull the covers off me. I opened my legs for him, squeezed my eyes tightly shut, felt his tongue flatten against my clit, and hoped he would, and wouldn't, do the g-spot thing again. I mean, I wouldn't have minded feeling it, but I wasn't trying to spend my entire honeymoon unconscious.

My *honeymoon*. Ain't that some shit?

"Mmmm," he moaned, as he worked some more of that coochie hoodoo with his tongue.

"Uh!" I whined, wiggling beneath him.

He licked and sucked me into an orgasm pretty quickly, then lifted from me, and asked, "You always come that quick?"

"Yeah, most of the time."

"Shit." Then he was in my face, my scent on his breath as he kissed me and then hovered over me, his eyes burning into mine. "I love the way you taste."

"Th-thank you."

"You still good with no condom like we discussed?"

"Yeah, we know each other's status, traded test results, and I'm on the pill so—ooooh, shit!"

He was inside me with one quick thrust, taking advantage of my orgasm-induced lubrication, and a little whimper escaped his mouth. His brow furrowed as he stared down at me, pulling back and sinking into me again.

"Damn, baby," he mumbled. "Shhhhhhit! You feel gooder than a motherfucker!"

I closed my eyes and tried to hold the orgasm that had literally started building on contact, but I couldn't and was soon contracting and spasming around him. "Neil!" I screamed in my daddy's voice. My daddy's *Liberian* voice. Shit, he was right!

"Shit! Shit! Shit! I'm not ready!" he screamed, sounding panicked.

"Oh, damn! I'm sorryyyyyyy! It's...just...so...good!"

He shut his eyes as if he was concentrating and kept going.

Grunting, moaning, whimpering, and kissing me as he worked my pussy like a damn physics equation, rocking in and out of me as orgasm after orgasm rolled over me.

"You making this hard for me, baby," he grunted. "I wanna stay in this good motherfucker, but I can't hold out any long—oh, fuck!"

He stiffened and grunted as I felt him grow and pulsate inside of me.

And then he collapsed onto my body, breathing heavily as he said, "Got damn."

As I awakened the next morning, the first thing I was aware of was his arms around me, and I smiled, snuggling closer to him and breathing in his scent. He felt and smelled so good, like a dream, but he was my reality now. He was my *husband*.

I heard him moan a little as he adjusted his body in the bed and loosened his grip on me, rubbing his hand up and down my back. "Mmm, grand rising, baby."

As my smile grew wider, I replied, "Grand rising, Neil."

15

Neil

I held her cheeks open and slid my tongue up the crack of her ass; then I squeezed one cheek while I bit the other.

She flinched, said, "Uh!" as I stood on my knees and rubbed the spot I'd bitten, sliding a finger inside her as the front of her body collapsed onto the bed and she pushed her ass toward me.

"Neil..." she moaned.

As I glided inside her, I reached down, grabbed a handful of her hair, and yanked her head back as I asked, "You got any idea how good this pussy is, Sage? I'm addicted to this shit."

"Oooo, Neil...Neil...Neil...Neil..."

I let her hair go and smacked her ass. "Yeah, baby. Feel it. Feel it, baby."

"Neil-Neil-Neil-Neil-Neil-Neeeeeeeil!" she screamed into the mattress.

She was coming already. It took all my strength not to bust on contact, because she was so hot and wet and I had been celibate for years; her milking the shit out of me didn't help the situation.

But this time, I just couldn't hold it, so I grabbed her ass cheeks and emptied into her with a, "Wooooo, shit!"

A few seconds later, I was lying on my back and Sage was next to me, still on her stomach, her eyes closed.

"Neil?" She sounded tired, but then again, she probably *was* tired. We'd been fucking all night off and on, into the morning. It was damn near noon, and we hadn't had a bite to eat since our wedding reception the day before. Hell, we both were probably dehydrated by now from all the sweating and coming we'd been doing. We were basically existing off of sex at that point.

"Yeah?" I replied.

"Why were you single before me? Why didn't you have a woman?"

"Why you ask that?"

She rolled over to face me, and my eyes instantly fell to her big, juicy breasts. I licked my lips and lifted my eyes to hers.

"Because I need to know why nobody been getting that good dick," she said.

That had me grinning. "Oh, so I wasn't just talking shit, huh?"

"Hell no!"

I chuckled. "Uh, after I broke up with the woman I had been with for like twelve years, I messed with a couple of women, but I was celibate for like seven, eight years until you. I was trying to deal with too much shit to deal with a woman, then. And why didn't you have a man, because that pussy is fire!"

"I had one, but..."

"What?"

"It's embarrassing. What happened between us is embarrassing."

"But you can tell me."

She didn't reply.

"If you tell me what happened with him, I'll tell you what happened with my ex, and I ain't never told no one about that. No one." *Huh? Did I just say that?*

"You will?"

"Uh...y-yeah."

She sighed, and her eyes left mine as she stared at something behind me. The wall, I guess. "Me and Gavin—

that's his name, Gavin Kowalski —"

"He's white?!" Damn, I didn't mean to yell that.

"No, I ain't never had sex with a white man, so you can calm your hotep ass down. He was adopted by some rich white people."

"Oh..."

"Anyway, we were together for like six months, lived together for five months, and things were going good. He was irresponsible as hell, wanted to be a thug but was really just a confused rebel against his parents, but he seemed to really care about me, you know? It took a while for me to get up the nerve, but eventually, I asked him if he'd help me out, if he'd marry me, and he said...he said he'd never marry me, that I wasn't the type of girl men marry. He said I was too loud and ghetto and fat, that I was the type you fuck until you find something better. Then he left, told me to get my shit out of his apartment and be gone when he got back. Mind you, we got the apartment together, but it was in his name. Still, I left. Left all my furniture there because I...I gave up. I was like, if the man I've been with all this time won't help me and would say that stuff to me, what's the use?" She looked at me and smiled. "Then you rescued me."

"What do you mean you gave up?" I asked.

"I...I thought about just ending it all. Gavin made me feel worthless, but not just him. Men have screwed me and dumped me before, treated me like a joke, and then there was the threat of deportation. I just...I didn't think life was worth living anymore."

I closed my eyes and shook my head. "I'm sorry you felt like that, but I'm glad you didn't do it. I'm glad you're here with me now."

"Me, too. Neil, some of the guys in my past said I was too touchy-feely. Like right now, I really wanna be up under you, but I don't wanna make you mad."

"The guys in your past were some asshole fuck boys. If you wanna touch me, anytime day or night, then you can touch me. I'm your husband, baby. My body is your body."

"And my body is your body?"

"Hell yeah."

She grinned as she scooted closer to me. "Your turn."

"Yeah, I did say that, huh?"

"Mm-hmm."

I wrapped my arm around her. "Me and Emery got together in junior high, stayed together through high school. I mean, we'd break up sometimes, fall out or whatever, but we always got back together. She followed me to Romey University in Tennessee; then she followed me to LA. We lived together in my house."

"The one you live in now?"

"The one *we* live in now."

"Yeah..."

"We were good, but I've always had a crazy sexual appetite—"

"No shit."

I laughed. "Yeah, and I've always liked exploring things, learning, and that didn't stop with sex. We tried everything, *anything*. She loved me, so if I thought it up, she'd do it. If I cheated, she forgave me. I asked for an open relationship, and she was cool with it. If I wanted to tie her up, she was down. If I wanted to fuck in a movie theater, she was with it. And when I asked for a threesome, she was game as long as she could choose the girl.

"Emery was a hair stylist, and she chose the woman who managed the salon she worked at, Gala, an older woman with a banging body. Shit, I was having so much fun with them, I didn't notice how much fun they were having with each other. After the first time, Emery started asking if we could do it again, and my dumb ass was excited, thinking how lucky I was that my woman was so open sexually, so willing to accommodate my needs. Three months after that first threesome, Emery announced to me that she was leaving me because she and Gala were in love. Baby, I was a man whose ego was built on his sexual prowess. I studied how to please women, read books on the g-spot, didn't feel satisfied unless I knew my partner had at least three orgasms, so that shit? It ripped a hole in my pride. She'd traded in my dick for a pussy!"

"Well, I'ma tell you right now. It didn't have a damn thing to do with your dick. On God, it didn't."

"I've had enough counseling to figure that much out, but thanks, baby, Anyway, not only was my ego destroyed, but at the same time, I was crushed by guilt. I'd taken advantage of her love for me, pushed her so far with my sexual exploration that I'd pushed her away. Still, I thought maybe this breakup was like the others and she'd come back to me. When she didn't, I lost myself. Started drinking to numb the pain, because as stupid as I was, I really did love her. Started gambling because…I don't know. I liked how it felt to win, made me feel like I wasn't a complete fuck-up, but the problem was, I didn't always win. Then one day, I looked up, years had passed, and my life was a fucking mess. Things were so fucked up, I couldn't see through the loss and pain to recognize the blessings I had. Ev's always been there for me. So has Leland. Nolan was my best friend growing up. My family loved me. I couldn't see any of that, though."

"What made you decide to turn your life around?"

"I got tired of being miserable, the family loser, but what really woke me up was seeing how happy Nolan was with your girl, Bridgette. I was like damn, Nolan found his queen? I mean, I love my brother, but he can be an asshole sometimes, an arrogant one. Then I looked at Ev, Leland, and Kat, all happily married, living their best lives…and I knew it was time for me to stop acting like my mama didn't raise me better than that."

"Thank you."

"For what?"

"For sharing that with me."

"You're welcome. Sage?"

"Yeah?"

"You ready for me to share some more of this dick with you?"

She climbed on top of me, giving me a slow kiss. "Like you said about me touching you, I'm your wife. If you want to give me this dick...give me this dick."

And I gave it to her like a motherfucker.

16

Sage

"You look good, baby. I like the way you tied that scarf on your head, and that dress? Damn!" he said into my ear, as I studied the menu in the hotel's restaurant.

"Thank you. You don't know how to act seeing me in clothes, do you?" I looked up at him with a raised eyebrow as he sat back in his seat and laughed.

"What you tryna say?" he asked.

I shrugged. "Nothing that you don't already know, like we've been here three days, and this is the first time we've stepped out of our suite. It's been nothing but sex, sleep, room service, sex, sex, shower with sex, room service, sleep, room service, sex while waiting for room service, sex because the sun rose, sex because there was a half-moon, room service, sleep…did I forget anything? Oh, yeah…sex!"

"I got a lot of catching up to do. You complaining?"

"You think I am?"

"I don't know. Maybe I need to start withholding some of that sex you're talking about."

"Really?"

"Shit, no."

I guffawed and then quickly covered my mouth. "My bad. I'm working on not being so loud in public."

"Be as loud as you want. I don't give a fuck what these white folks think."

"I guess being married to a woke man has its advantages."

"You know it."

After the waiter finally came and took our orders, I said, "Since we are now married and have had sex three hundred and sixty-two-point-seven times, I think we should get to know each other better."

"I already told you what happened with my ex. My family doesn't even know that."

"And I appreciate that, but I wanna know more."

"Okay…what you wanna know?"

"What do you like to do besides read and fuck?"

He laughed again. "Uh…I like to listen to music."

"For real?" I chirped. "Who's your favorite artist?"

"Hmm, it's a tie between Common and Mos Def."

"Why does that not surprise me?"

He shrugged. "Who's yours?"

"Big-motherfucking-South! The GOAT of rap! Who else?"

He grinned. "Is that right? You like my brother, huh?"

"Yes! Can't nobody touch him as far as I'm concerned. If I didn't know you were woke and stuff, I would've expected him to be your favorite, too."

"He is. I didn't think I needed to say that. Mos Def and Common come after him, of course."

"What's your favorite Big South song?" I asked.

He tapped his fingers on the table for a few seconds, and said, "*Panty Gag.*"

"Yeah, that's a bop for sure. But my fave is *Stop and Frisk.* Now, that's a classic!"

"Yeah, but I wrote the music for *Panty Gag*, so…"

"That's right! You did! Wow, you've got talent, Neil!"

"I do all right. So, what else you wanna know about me?"

"Why are you hotep?"

"Well, because ever since I was little, I didn't understand why everything we learned was so…white. We're taught that classical music is white, classical art is white, classical dance is ballet—white. All the great thinkers—white, but the first university was built by Africans in Africa. Shidddd, let our oppressors tell it, the Africans or the Chinese or anyone from civilizations that came before white civilization didn't do shit. Do you know that at one point they tried to say Egyptians were black-skinned white people? I mean, that shit was an accepted fact! They stay stealing stuff and taking credit for creating it. I just ain't never bought into that Eurocentric bullshit."

"That's why you hate white people?"

"I don't hate white people, I hate white supremacy. I hate white lies and not the innocent lies they label as white lies. You see how perverse that shit is? A white lie is an innocent lie? What the fuck is an innocent lie? That shit don't exist. But that's what they do…they make stuff benefit them. They stole this land, then made it illegal to steal. They murdered all them damn Native Americans and then made murder illegal. They lie, but when they lie, it's okay. Everybody else lies and it's perjury. Naw, I don't hate white people; I just don't fear them or believe everything they try to feed us, and I'm committed to furthering *my* race, a race a lot of them seem to want to exterminate. I ain't one of them niggas who talks black and fucks white, because that shit is backwards as hell to me. Them niggas are breeding themselves out and ain't got sense enough to see it. And all they can say is black women are too difficult to be with. What kinda weak beta male shit is that?"

"Uh…"

"Sorry, I didn't mean to go on a tangent, but it's a lot of shit that bothers me."

"It's okay. You're just…passionate. I bet Nolan dating all those Ukrainians really got under your skin."

"Yeah, that was problematic as hell for me, but he got his self together, and I'm glad. But unlike him, it was always my plan to marry a black woman and have black kids. Just didn't know you'd be my wife."

With inflated eyes, I asked, "You wanna have kids with me?"

"You're my wife. Who else I'ma have 'em with?"

I didn't have an answer for that, so I said, "Um, is everything you read hotep stuff?"

"Mostly, but let's do this right. Hotep has become a derogatory term, and although I use it sometimes because it has a good meaning, I actually subscribe to black empowerment and truth and gaining knowledge of self. I'm all about us loving ourselves for who we are as black people and embracing our skin, our hair, and our own culture without seeing it as inferior to white culture so that we can reach our full potential as a people. Using our own beauty as the standard and not theirs, our own greatness as a metric. I *was* a part of the black consciousness community, but I take issue with some of my conscious brothers."

"Why?" I asked, taking a sip of my water.

"Well, in the past, I loved a black woman, but did not respect her. Neither did any of the brothers in the movement. They place blame on our queens for every-damn-thing, and most of the shit is our fault. We're supposed to be leading, right? So if shit is fucked up, it's on us. Ain't nothing conscious or woke about a black man disrespecting black women, and I will never do it again."

"I see."

We paused our conversation as the waiter placed our plates in front of us, and as I cut into my chicken parmesan, Neil said, "Sage, let's fall in love."

I looked up to see him staring at me, his pasta primavera still sitting before him untouched. "What?" I asked, but I'd heard him loud and clear.

"Let's fall in love."

"You make it sound like it's so simple for you. Real, reciprocated love isn't that simple."

"Yes, it is. All we gotta do is let it happen."

"You really want to? You want to fall in love with me?"

"At this point, I think it's inevitable, baby."

I stared off into the distance and nodded. "Okay, then I'll

let it happen."

He smiled at me. "Asé."

"Asé," I returned.

I don't know why, but even with my horrible history when it came to love, I believed that if by some miracle we did fall in love, real love, it would work out. Maybe his confidence in us having a real marriage was rubbing off on me.

"Hey, what does hotep mean?" I asked.

"Peace."

"Would you teach me more stuff?"

"You mean consciousness stuff?"

I nodded. "Yeah, I can't be sleep when I'm married to a woke man."

He chuckled. "Word? Well, you're an entrepreneur. That's woke as fuck, baby."

"For real?"

"Yeah, you ain't on that corporate plantation. No slave master, no boss to answer to but you."

"So, I guess I'm not totally asleep. Just groggy, huh?"

Smiling, he said, "Yeah, I guess you are."

"I still wanna learn from you, though."

"Okay, let's see. Well, first of all…did you know the original name for The Continent was Nubia and not Africa?"

"No, I didn't."

"Yeah, and…"

*****

With my head on his chest in the darkness of our suite, I asked, "What's your favorite color?"

"Black," he answered.

"Should've figured that."

He chuckled. "What's yours? White?"

"You know it. Favorite food?"

"Sweet potatoes. Yours?"

"My mom's chicken gravy. It'll make you hurt yourself!"

"Word? Can you make it?"

"Yeah. I can cook most of the stuff she makes, but I can't promise it'll be as good as hers."

"You gonna cook for me sometimes?"

"You want me to?"

"Yeah, I'd love for you to."

"Okay, I will...favorite movie? *Black Panther*? *Malcolm X*? *Get Out*?"

"So you think I'm that one-dimensional?"

"No..."

"Well, my favorite movie is *The Wiz*."

I lifted my head and tried to see his face. "*The Wiz*? Are you serious?"

"Yeah...it was my mom's favorite movie. She'd watch it all the time when I was little, and I grew to love it because of the memories attached to it."

"Wow, that's beautiful. She was a good woman. I can tell that from the way you and your siblings are. She raised some good kids."

"Yeah, my mama was the best woman in the world. I think about her all the time, see her in my dreams. I miss the shit out of her, my daddy, too. So enough mushy stuff. What's *your* favorite movie?"

"*Just Wright* with Queen Latifah and Common."

"Yeah? Never seen that one."

"It's basically a fairy tale love story where the big girl gets the guy. I guess that's always been a fantasy for me. Never thought it'd come true, but here I am with you, coochie vibrating from the punishment you just put on it. Dreams do come true!"

He laughed, tightening his arms around me. "Shit, you're a dream come true, too. Got me thinking about tatting Superdick up. I'ma get 'Property of Sage' on him."

"Really? Shoot, I would get 'Neil's Playground' on my yoni if I wasn't afraid of pain."

"You ain't gotta do that, but what you *can* do is ride this dick."

"Say no more."

Neil

"Neil? Or Nolan? Hiiiii!"

I'd know that voice anywhere.

I stopped in my tracks, ice bucket in hand, and turned around to face her. Esther Reese, Everett's first wife, was ambling sloppily down the hotel's hallway with the help of Dunn—Everett's former bodyguard. He was working for Esther now? What was this dude doing, trying to work for all my brother's enemies?

"It's Neil. What's up, Esther? Dunn?"

Dunn gave me a nod, and Esther slurred in that accent of hers, "Oh, you know…just having fun. Here celebrating."

"Celebrating what?"

"I'm the newest member of the *Real Divas of LA* cast!"

Damn, that show was ratchet as hell, a big drop from *Go See*. "Congrats."

"Thank you!"

"Is Ella here with you?"

"No, she's with your brother and his ugly little wife. Did I hear you got married? Congratulations!"

"Uh, thanks. We're actually here on our honeymoon."

"Awwww! Let me give you a hug." She reached for me and almost fell.

Dunn caught her, and said, "I got you."

"Oh, thank you, Ashley!"

Ashley? Dunn's first name is Ashley?

"Neil, it was good to see you. I'm going to go to my room so me and Ashley can have sex now. I am going to suck him dry! Byyyyyye!"

"Yeah, cheerio or whatever," I mumbled.

With my eyes bugged like a motherfucker, I went to my room and was going to tell Sage what'd just happened, but she was lying on her stomach staring at her phone, naked and uncovered with only a strand of red beads around her waist, and well, fuck Esther. I had more pressing business to take care of.

17

$\mathcal{S}age$

"Where'd you get those red beads you had around your waist?" he asked, leaning in close to me.

"They were a gift from Leland's wife, Kim. She gave them to me at my shower. You like them?" I shouted over the music.

"Mm-hmm. I'ma buy you some more."

"Well, thank you. Hey, you know what fantasy I have?"

His face was in my neck as he said, "No, tell me."

I moved my head a bit and looked at him. Damn, he looked good even in that horrible club lighting. This was our last night in Palm Springs, and I'd made him take me out. Otherwise, I would've been in that bed in that hotel room throwing my ass back at him. Not that I had a problem with that, but shit, I wanted to have something to share with my friends about this honeymoon when we got back.

"This one time, at *Vault*," I began, "there was this couple straight fucking at their booth. They weren't naked, and of course it was dark in there, but she was in his lap and you could tell what was happening. And it was like they got lost in it, forgot anyone was around or that they were in a nightclub. That was so hot to me."

"So, you wanna have sex in a club? That's your fantasy?"

I shrugged. "A club or just in public, I guess. But with the music and atmosphere, a club would be my first pick."

"Hmm..."

"Neil?"

His mouth was on my neck again as he hummed, "Mmm?"

"This was a good honeymoon. It felt...it felt real. You made it feel real."

He lifted his head and looked me in the eye. "It *is* real, baby. I'm real, you're real, all that good-ass sex we had was real, our conversations are real, and it's gonna keep being real. And if I gotta lick your ass, suck your clit, and screw you into believing that, I will. We're falling in love, remember?"

Shit, I'm already halfway there. "Yeah, I remember."

"Keep remembering it," he said, and leaned in to kiss me as Summer Walker's *CPR* blasted from the club's speakers.

*****

"You feel it, baby? You feel that?"

Neil was in my ear and in my vagina, one hand gripping my hip and the other gripping my hair as I held onto the kitchen counter, my jeans on the floor by my feet, my blouse pushed up my back. We'd just made it back home from our honeymoon, had barely made it inside the house, and this happened. I mean, I walked into the kitchen to check and see if my pineapple juice was still good — yeah, I kept that on deck; my levels were on fleek — and the next thing I knew, Neil was on me, talking about how he'd been horny the whole ride home. Then he yanked my jeans down without unbuttoning or unzipping them, licked my actual ass, and was now screwing the living shit out of me.

Damn, this was Heaven.

"Oh, Neil! Neil!"

"Yeah, baby...feel that shit!"

"I feel it! I feel it! I feeeeeeel iiiiiiiit!" The orgasm rolled through me, and I collapsed onto the counter. He wasn't far behind me, and soon, I was bearing his weight on the back of my body and feeling his heavy breaths on the nape of my neck.

I was trying to catch my own breath when the doorbell rang. "That's got to be Jo or Bridgette or both. They were blowing my phone up the whole time we were in Palm Springs."

He lifted off me. "Why didn't you answer?"

"I was too busy having sex with my husband."

"Oh, yeah...that's right. I'll get the door," he said with a grin, as he pulled his pants up and left the kitchen.

As I gathered myself, I heard both my friends enter the house, heard them greet him and ask about me.

I entered the living room to find Bridgette and Jo on the sofa, and said, "Hey, hookers!"

"Don't 'hey hookers' us! We were worried to death!" Bridgette yelled.

"Uh, I'ma let y'all talk," Neil said.

"Naw, brother-in-law. I got a bone to pick with you, too." Bridgette stopped him in his tracks.

"Huh?" Poor Neil was confused as hell.

"Just because y'all decided to make it a real honeymoon by screwing all over Palm Springs doesn't mean you get to ignore our calls!" Bridgette accurately accused.

"What?!" both me and Neil shouted.

"And don't bother denying it. Y'all just finished screwing. I know you did, because Neil's got that same 'I just got some pussy' look on his face that Nolan wears after we have sex. Damn, y'all look exactly alike!" Bridgette informed us.

Neil raised his thick eyebrows. "Well, we're identical twins, so..."

"And I had Ev call you when I couldn't get Sage, Neil. You had your phone off! I thought you two were killing each other or something!" Jo fussed.

"Well, he *was* killing this pussy," I mumbled.

Neil held up his hands. "Okay, look...I understand your concern for Sage, because y'all are close, but she's my wife now. I got her."

Silence from my friends.

"I do! We're good," he said, with a huge grin on his face.

"I can see that. She's glowing. Damn, y'all move quick," Bridgette expressed. "I thought this would take at least six months."

"Huh?" I said.

"I told you. I could see it at the wedding. I *knew* they liked each other," Jo said.

"Here, bitch." Bridgette dug in her purse and handed Jo a hundred-dollar bill that she quickly snatched from her.

"Wow, y'all placing bets on us? That's fucked up," Neil said. "Y'all do know I'm a recovering gambler, right?"

"Oh...our bad," Bridgette said.

"Y'all some treacherous wenches," I interjected.

"Whatever. Now that we know you two aren't dead but just freaks, we'll leave y'all to it. Bye!" Bridgette waved at us as she and Jo let themselves out.

Then Neil looked at me and shook his head. "Ain't that some shit?"

"Yep, those fools need to stop."

"They really do. I'm horny again."

"Me, too."

"Come on. Let's go christen the bed."

18

Neil

The marriage...

"Mr. McClain? There's a customer who wants to speak to the person in charge, and since Jackie's not here, I figured that would be you."

Looking up from the computer screen, I frowned slightly. Jennifer looked frazzled. "Did they say what it's about? What's going on?"

Jennifer shrugged. "It's about some book we don't have in stock? I did a search of our wholesaler's inventory, then a general web search, and I can't find it. I think she might have the title wrong, but when I suggested that, she got angry, asked for a manager."

I sighed as I stood and stretched. "All right. Let's see what I can do."

As I followed her to the front of the store, a part of me hoped it was Sage playing a trick on me or something, but I knew she was doing makeup for a wedding — the bride and fifteen bridesmaids. So there was no way it was her. Still, the thought of her made me smile. We'd been married for two weeks, had a good little rhythm going, and other than the fact that she left her shoes in the middle of the bedroom floor and my ass was always tripping over them, life with her was good. Sage was funny, silly, more youthful than her age, and I honestly think I needed that. I was serious, too serious sometimes, and I could admit that. Being woke could wear on a person, make them too sober for their own good. No pun intended.

That smile I was wearing faded when Jennifer pointed the customer out to me. She didn't look disgruntled at all when she saw me. She was wearing a huge smile, and as I approached her, said, "It's been a while, huh?"

A lot of shit shot through my mind, things like how she'd been the one to cut off contact with me, and how she'd asked Nolan to talk to me, to tell me to leave her alone. How she'd changed her number, and how fucking devastated I was to lose her even if the shit was my fault. But instead of any of that, I said, "Yeah. Uh, what can I help you with? What was the title of the book you were asking about?"

Emery gave me a sheepish look. "Actually, I made the title of the book up. I just wanted to see you."

"How'd you know I was here?"

"I didn't."

My cell buzzed in my pocket, and as I took it out to check it, she said, "I ran into Jeremy Unger the other day, and he told me how good you're doing. You look great, Neil."

I read Sage's *What you doing?* message and smiled. "Thanks," I said, without looking up at Emery.

Then I replied to Sage's text: *Wish I was doing you.*

I vaguely heard Emery say, "Um, you wanna grab a coffee? Chat for a bit?"

Sage: *Well, the damn wedding was canceled, so guess where I'm headed?*

Me: *You better be heading home and getting naked.*

Sage: *You read my mind! You gonna come get you some of this hot and ready pepperoni pussy, Mr. Vegan?*

I chuckled. She stayed incorrectly calling me a vegan.

"Neil? Did you hear me?" Emery asked.

Shit, I forgot she was standing there. "Yeah. Hey, I gotta go. It was nice seeing you."

"That was a text from your wife? Jeremy told me you got

married."

I nodded. "Yep."

"Oh."

"See you around, Emery." Without waiting for her to respond, I told Jennifer I was leaving for the day and typed out my response to Sage as I walked out the door.

Me: *Baby, you know I'm a coochie carnivore.*

*****

I popped up in the bed. The last time I had a dream like that was the night before I agreed to marry Sage, and just like that dream, she was in it. Why did I keep calling them dreams? They were the definition of a nightmare, the kind of shit that made me sweat and shudder.

In the darkness of the bedroom, I reached for her to reassure myself she was okay, but she wasn't there, so I called her name.

No answer.

What the fuck?

I got up and searched the whole house. Checked the driveway and saw that her car was gone. It was after midnight. So I went back to the bedroom, grabbed my phone, and called her.

"Hello?!" she yelled into the phone. "Neil?"

I could hear music and people. Was she at a motherfucking club? "Where the fuck you at?!" I barked.

"Hold on!" There was a pause, the music died down, and then she said, "Okay, I'm back. What'd you say?"

"I said, where the fuck you at?!"

"Uh...at Ramona's."

"Ramona's, as in the strip club? What in the fuck are you

doing there?"

"Chocolate Shaker's makeup." She said the shit like it made perfect sense for her to leave the damn house in the middle of the night without telling me.

"And what the hell is a chocolate shaker?"

"She's a friend of mine. That's her stripper name. Her real name is Minnie. Anyway, after Sticky Vicky saw how I did Chocolate's makeup, she asked me to do hers. Then Red Snapper asked me to do hers. I'm working on her face right now. Then I gotta do Bust it Wide Open's face."

"Oh, I see." I hung up the damn phone, threw on a damn Kufi hat and a damn track suit jacket with my pajama pants, slipped on some damn Nike sandals, and jumped in my damn car. When I made it to Ramona's, the bouncer had the nerve to look me up and down and tell me I couldn't get in without a shirt.

To that, I said, "Then I need you to go to wherever the strippers get their makeup done and tell the chick with the braids to bring her ass outside. I'm her husband."

"You talking 'bout little Sage?" he asked, sounding too damn familiar for my liking.

"Little Sage?!" I questioned, with my eyebrows up in my brain.

Then the big motherfucker said, "Hold on a sec. I'll tell her you're here."

About five minutes later, Sage walked outside in some damn shorts, showing her thigh meat and shit. "Neil? What are you doing here? Why'd you hang up on me? Where's your shirt? Damn, you're fine..."

I scratched my chin and gave her a backwards nod. "Come here. Let me holler at you for a minute."

With confusion in her eyes, she inched closer to me. "Neil, what's going on?"

"That's what I need to know."

"Huh?"

"You wanna explain to me why my motherfucking wife left

my bed in the middle of the got-damn night to do stripper makeup in a got-damn strip club in got-damn booty shorts without saying a got-damn word to me? Huh?"

"These ain't booty shorts."

I stared at her.

"Uh, I didn't wanna wake you up, and when Chocolate called, I didn't wanna turn down the money since I missed the money I would've made off the wedding gig."

"Go get your shit."

"But—why?"

"Because it's the middle of the night! You shouldn't be here! What you tryna pay? Credit cards? Student loans? A car note? I got you. But this ain't gonna work for me. Go get your shit so we can go the-fuck home, Sage."

"Neil—" Her eyes scanned the area around us. The bouncer was staring at us, a couple of the strippers were watching us from the door, and I didn't give a shit. "Neil…"

"Sage? You okay, girl?" one of the strippers yelled from the door.

"She good," I answered. Then I dropped my eyes back to my wife. "Go get your shit and let's go, Sage. *Now.*"

Sage sighed and dropped her shoulders. "I'll be right back."

She followed me home in her car, stormed inside the house, and threw her keys on the coffee table in the living room. "I can't believe you showed up at that club with your damn chest out acting a pure fool! That was fucking embarrassing, Neil!"

"I woke up and you were gone! You scared the shit outta me! Something could've happened to you, Sage! Going out in the middle of the night like that is dangerous!"

She fell onto the sofa. "Ain't nobody gonna mess with me. I've been doing this a long time. Shit, most people look right through me. I'm invisible."

"Not to me. You're my rib!"

She shook her head. "Well, I've always done stuff like this and no man ever seemed to care."

I sat down beside her. "I ain't them."

"I know. I know you care, but did you have to curse me out in front of the club?"

"I'm sorry. I just…like I said, you scared me. Don't do no shit like that again, okay?"

She sighed. "Okay."

"And no more strip clubs. My money is not tight. I just got a royalty check for the work I did on the *Mrs. South* EP. If you need something, tell me. Hell, your name is on my account. If you need something, take it!"

"I thought you just added me to your account for my green card paperwork."

"No! I added you to my account and the deed to this house and my store because you're my wife! Look, just don't do no shit like this again. Ever. *Please.*"

"I-I won't."

"And don't leave this house in no damn Daisy Dukes again, either."

"These aren't that short. You're exaggerating."

"Sage McClain, I am not playing with you. Don't leave this house with your thigh meat showing again unless I'm with you. You gonna make me get arrested."

Shaking her head, she said, "Fine."

He'd already left the bed when I woke up the next morning feeling a whole lot of stuff—still embarrassed, but also treasured. He was seriously upset about me leaving without telling him. His reaction further solidified the fact that the men in my past were some certified dingleberries. Hell, my fake husband actually cared more about my well-being than my authentic boyfriends ever did. I guess this thing was really...real.

I was sitting on the side of the bed, checking my phone and answering a text from Chocolate Shaker, when Neil peeked his head in the bedroom door.

"Good, you're up. Come have breakfast with me. I gotta go to the bookstore in a little bit," he said.

I nodded and headed to the kitchen in my t-shirt and panties.

As I sat down at the table, he set a plate in front of me. "Sweet potato pancakes."

"You made these? We ain't got no sweet potatoes," was my response.

"I went to the store this morning."

"Oh...you want me to give you the money for them since the groceries are my thing?"

"Don't worry about it."

"Okay...we got syrup?"

"Yep."

After I drowned them in syrup, I dug into the best damn pancakes I'd ever tasted! When I was done, I chugged my water, and said, "That was so good!"

"You like that, huh? You want seconds?"

I shook my head. "Maybe later."

He nodded, cleared our plates from the table, and said, "Stand up."

"Uh, why?" I asked.

"You'll see."

So I stood, and he pushed my chair back. When he picked me up and sat me on the table, I shrieked, "Neil! What—"

"Lay back."

"What are you—"

"Baby, lay back."

I lay back, my eyes on the ceiling as he opened my legs, moved my panties to the side and covered my whole damn pussy with his mouth.

"Oh!" I yelled. "Oh! Oh! Oh!"

"Mmm, mm-hmm…hmm…ummmmmmm," he replied, as his tongue swirled around my clit.

When his mouth left me and he slid his fingers inside me and started stroking that spot, I damn near jumped off the table. "Neil…Neil, wait. Shit!" It felt so good, but it was too much, and I wasn't sure if I could take it, but I wanted it, but I was scared of it.

He massaged my clit with his thumb, kept his fingers rubbing my g-spot, and asked, "You want me to stop?"

"Shit!"

"That ain't an answer, baby."

"Noooooooo! Don't sto—ohhhhhh, got-damn!"

It hit me. Not a wave but an avalanche, an eight-point-zero earthquake of pleasure, and my whole body started vibrating again. I felt him lift me from the table and hold me in his arms, and I started crying. It was too damn much!

"You look so beautiful when you come for me…you know that? Beautiful, baby," he said into my ear.

I couldn't stop crying. I tried, but I just couldn't stop.

He rubbed my head, told me it was okay, kissed me, and held me until I finally calmed down.

Through a sniffle, I said, "I don't understand what just happened."

"You had an orgasm."

"I know that, but…I'm sorry for last night, Neil. I'm so sorry," I whimpered.

"No, *I'm* sorry. I shouldn't have come at you like that or yelled at you, cursed at you. That was disrespectful, and you might be younger than me, but you're not a child. It's just that

I had this dream that you were hurt, that someone was hurting you, and the shit scared me. Then I woke up and you were gone, and I didn't know where you were or if you were safe. Can't nothing happen to you, you hear me? I can't let nothing happen to you."

"Neil...this morning, I-I got a text from Choc—Minnie. She said someone came in there with a gun after I left. One of the dancers' boyfriends came in there threatening to shoot up the place and actually got some shots off in the dancers' dressing room before security tackled him. No one was hurt, but she said it was good you made me leave. So thank you. Even if you were rough about it, you probably saved my life."

He sighed and clutched me tighter. "I got you, baby. I promise I do, and I always will."

19

Sage

"I'll have the strawberry and spinach salad. Thanks," I said, handing the waiter my menu.

After he'd left our table, Jo took a sip of her water, and said, "I'm so glad we sisters-in-law could get together today, and especially since Kim is in town."

"Me, too! I never get to hang with y'all since we're in St. Louis most of the time!" Kim chirped.

"Or on the road. Leland be dragging you all over the place!" Bridgette observed.

"Yeah, he swears something is gonna happen to me if I'm not with him damn near every hour of the day," Kim said, rolling her eyes.

"Those damn McClain boys are so overprotective! Geez!" Jo said, glancing at the table next to ours where three security guards sat. Two for her and one for Kim.

"I know mine is," I kind of mumbled.

"Speaking of yours…how are things going with you and Neil?" Jo asked.

"Good. I mean, it's an adjustment, but we're making it work," I replied.

"I've always liked Neil, although he's usually quiet around me. I knew he'd be a good man once he got himself together," Kim shared.

"Mm-hmm," Bridgette said, "and I bet you getting fucked like you stole something from him and refused to give it back. I can only imagine the savagery he's putting down in the bedroom!"

Kim's mouth fell open.

"Wow," I said.

"Really, Bridge?" Jo interjected. "You do know you're talking about your husband's twin, right?

"Yeah...and?"

"You are so damn crazy."

"So, you're gonna sit over there and act like you haven't been thinking the same thing? Shit, you *know* she getting it good!" Bridgette declared.

Jo rolled her eyes and then fixed them on me. "As crude as Bridgette is, uh...is it savage? We're family for real, now. You can tell us."

"Y'all are too funny," Kim commented.

I shrugged. "I mean, yeah. It's the best sex I've ever had in my life."

Bridgette offered me her hand for a high-five. "I knew it! I can just look at him and see all that pent-up black rage and hotep hostility, and I know he's a damn pussy annihilator!"

After I smacked her hand, I said, "Girrrrrl, you just don't know. I'm sprung as hell. Whew, chillay!"

"Okay, now that we have established that good sex is a McClain dominant trait—" Jo began, but was interrupted by Bridgette, who said, "How do we know Leland is good in bed?"

All eyes were on Kim.

"I gave that man a baby when my only child at the time was twenty years old. What does that tell you?" she said.

"That he got the magic stick, too!" Bridgette avowed.

"And you know it!" Kim agreed.

"Lord, help us all. Anyway," Jo continued, "how are things otherwise? Outside the bedroom, I mean."

I sighed. "Good, when I'm not doing stupid shit to make

him mad."

Bridgette frowned. "Like what?'

After I explained what happened with me and the strip club, Jo said, "Yeah, I know that upset him. I think maybe you were operating like this was still an arrangement that didn't involve feelings, but he definitely has feelings for you to react like that. Are y'all all right now, though?"

"Yeah, he apologized for going off on me in front of the club, and I apologized for leaving like that without letting him know, and the next morning, he made me pancakes and ate my coochie on the kitchen table, so we're good. Plus, he gave me one of those g-spot orgasms that make me feel like I'm on another planet. Then, later that night, he ate my pussy and ass while we were in the shower, and we had sex like three times before we went to sleep. So, we're cool now."

After they stared at me for a full five minutes, all three of them simultaneously said, "Daaaaaamn."

Neil

"What you up to, man?" Nolan asked, his voice booming from my SUV's speakers.

"'Bout to head into the Sankofa Center," I replied, my eyes glued to the house where I got my life back on track.

"Counseling session?"

"Yep. But she's talking about releasing me soon."

"That's good, man. Real good."

"Thanks, thanks."

"So, I wanted to call and let you know I'm proud of you, Neil. For real. You really turned things around. I mean, it's like I got my original brother back."

"Instead of the fucked-up one you were ashamed of?"

"I wasn't never ashamed of you, man. Just wanted you to do better, That's all. I know you, Neil, and your potential. I know better than anyone how brilliant your mind is. I just wanted you to be the best you could be."

"What the fuck you supposed to be now? An army recruiter?"

"Oh, your ass got jokes, huh? See, I wasn't gonna mess with you about what my wife said about you and your wife over there screwing like a couple of possessed rabbits, but since you wanna start shit…"

"Yeah, I'm screwing the living daylights outta my woman…and?"

"Oh, shit! So it's on for real, huh?"

"Yep, and I'm enjoying every minute of it."

"Good. Sounds like she is, too."

"Hell, I *know* she is."

"Yeah, my original brother is definitely back."

"I would ask you how married life is treating you, but I can see that it's treating you well," she said, with a warm smile on her face.

I nodded, shifting my eyes from that Sankofa painting to her face. "Yeah. I mean, it's different, but I love it. She's…she's everything you said she was. She can be a piece of work because she's a hustler, real independent, but I feel good with her in a way I've never experienced before. She makes me want to be better and better. I'm not sure if either of us was really prepared for what it takes to keep a marriage together, but I'm willing to put in the work."

Mother Erica leaned forward and clasped her hands as she

often did, her eyes on me as she said, "That's love. Even in its infancy, love takes work, but it's work you don't mind doing, because you know the benefits outweigh the effort. Neil, when you first came here all broken and frustrated with yourself and your life, my first thought was that you needed love. Your heart needed the exercise, your soul needed the sacrifice, and your body needed the kind of healing only good loving can provide. And look at you now."

I turned my head, gazing out of the big window in her office with a smile on my face. "Yeah...look at me now."

*****

"Aw, shit! Turn up time!!! It's my king's earthstrong in this bitch! Where's the sparkling grape juice?!" Sage yelled, as we entered *Second Avenue* for the birthday party Bridgette was throwing for Nolan. I was invited by default, but whatever. I was just glad to be there with Sage. Two months of marriage, and I knew I'd follow her ass anywhere. She was a real blessing. Gave me something to care about, something to cherish, a reason to wake up in the morning.

Sage grabbed my hand and pulled me toward the dancefloor. "Come on, baby. Let's dance!"

As luck would have it, Drake's *In My Feelings* had ended by the time we hit the floor, and Ella Mai's *Trip* began to play, so I pulled my queen into my arms and buried my face in her neck as we moved to the song. I licked and kissed her neck, rubbed her booty, and jumped when I heard my name blasted through the speakers.

"Damn, Neil! I know y'all newlyweds, but shit!"

Leland.

Sage was laughing as I looked toward the DJ booth and

threw my middle finger up at my little brother. All my brothers were some assholes. For real.

My family congregated in one of the roped-off VIP areas, so we could be in the middle of the action. All five of the McClain siblings and our spouses filled couches and roasted each other. Well, I was the subject of most of the roasting because I couldn't keep my hands off my wife, but whatever. I didn't care. I just laughed, because the shit was funny.

"Damn, Sage. What you doing to him? Nigga over there smiling and shit," Everett said.

"And look at him. She tried to sit next to him and he pulled her on his lap, keeps rubbing her thighs and stuff!" That was Nolan. "What you tryna do, get in a speedy out here or something?"

"Quickie, baby. It's called a quickie," Bridgette corrected him.

"Oh, yeah...that," Nolan said.

"I bet her pineapple levels are off the charts!" Leland shouted.

"Ain't you supposed to be somewhere dribbling a basketball?" I quipped. Truthfully though, I'd heard about the pineapple thing years earlier, and yes, my baby's levels were at one hundred and ten percent at all times.

"The season is over, shithead, and you know it. And I'm glad I made it, so I can see what it looks like for your Malcolm X ass to be all in love and shit."

"Wait a minute, what are pineapple levels?" Kat asked. I was surprised she and Tommy made it. She hated leaving little Randy with a sitter, and she still stayed keeping Leland Jr. all the time, too.

"Ain't nobody telling you about that. Hell naw!" Ev shouted.

"I got you, girl. I'll text you the details," Kim said.

"You better the-fuck not!" Leland yelled.

"Oh, shut up, Leland Randall!" Kat fussed.

"I can't be happy without y'all fucking with me?" I asked,

kissing Sage's arm.

"Look at your ass. You just can't help yourself, can you?" Nolan asked.

"Hey, Nole...fuck you," was my response.

"What I'm tripping on is what you told us about Esther and Dunn, though. Like, wow!" Bridgette interjected.

"I ain't surprised. She always did have a thing for bodyguard dick. But now I know I gotta get Ella out that house. I don't like the fact that Dunn is hanging around her. I don't trust his ass," Everett said.

"Shit, neither do I," Jo agreed.

"Neil?"

The hairs on the back of my neck stood up, and my head shot up to see Emery standing beside the couch Sage and I occupied. How the hell did she get past all of Everett's and Leland's security?

My family cleared out of that space so fast, the shit almost made me dizzy. As they made their exits, they all mumbled shit like, "Oh, hell. I'm out."

Sage gave me a confused look, so I made the introductions. "Emery Bledsoe—I guess it's still Bledsoe—this is my wife, Sage. Sage, this is Emery...my ex."

Sage tightened her arms around my neck. "Oh...hi."

"Hi, great to meet you!" Emery gushed.

"Uh-huh. Um, Neil, I'ma go to the bathroom," Sage said.

"Okay." I kissed her and swatted her booty when she stood from my lap. "Hurry your sexy ass back."

"I will."

Sage left, and Emery took it upon herself to sit down next to me. "Happy earthday, Neil."

"Uh, thanks."

"Your wife is cute."

"You were invited?" I asked, wondering why this woman suddenly kept popping up after years of no contact. Bridgette had organized everything. Did she invite her?

"No, my friend was. She had a small part in *Floetic Lustice*.

She invited me to tag along."

Or did you invite yourself? "Hmm."

Her hand met my knee, and she smiled at me. "You know…I've missed you."

I squinted at her and stood from the couch. "Let me go find my wife. Good seeing you, Emery."

"Wait! Neil, wait! I need to talk to you."

I sighed and shook my head. "About what?"

"Us and—"

"Did I make you wait too long?" Sage appeared, stepping over Emery and wrapping her arms around me. "You miss me?"

"Yeah. You know I did."

She reached up and bit the front of my neck, and I laughed. "You tryna take my moves from me?" I asked.

"You only bite my ass."

"Oh, let me fix that." I bit her neck, and she giggled. Then our mouths locked for a good five minutes. When we came up for air, Emery was gone.

"Oh, shit! This is my jam!" Sage screamed, pulling on my hand and leading me back down to the dancefloor where we smiled and danced to Jacquees' and Dej Loaf's *At the Club*.

$\mathcal{S}age$

Emery Bledsoe, owner/operator of Natural Knots Beauty Salon, specializing in braids and natural hair maintenance. Divorced. No kids. Lives in Los Felix.

Bitch.

The next morning, I paid for an internet background check on this bitch, because she was getting too close for comfort. When I saw her sitting next to Neil in *Second Avenue*, I almost fucked her up on-sight. He was *my* man, dammit! She'd had her chance!

"What you looking at? You always on that computer," Neil said, sitting next to me on the sofa, where he was, of course, reading a book.

"You still don't have a TV, so what do you expect me to do?"

"You want me to get one? Just tell me."

I slammed the computer shut. "No, I don't want a got-damn TV, Neil." I slung my laptop onto the recliner, and hopped to my feet, stomping to the kitchen where I started opening and slamming cabinet doors shut like a lunatic.

"I don't want her, I didn't invite her, and I have no idea why she was there," he said, scaring the shit out of me. I didn't know he'd followed me.

"She was there because she sees that you got yourself together and you're fine as fuck and now she wants you back! You know that's what it is!" I screamed.

"Okay, maybe that's true. But it takes two, and my heart belongs to you, baby. I don't want her."

"I'd understand if you did. She's pretty, really pretty. And thin. She could be a model if she was taller. Was that her hair? And her eyes...they were gray. Are those her eyes? And she seems real cultured. I see why you were so heartbroken over losing her. I'm nothing like her."

"Sage—"

"I mean, it's been good, better than good, but I'll be okay if you wanna give things with her another shot. I was gonna suck your dick for your birthday, but after I saw her, I was like, she probably sucks dick better than me, and if I do it, it'll only remind you of her, so..."

"Sage, baby—"

"And I got you a gift. I forgot to give it to you. Are you gonna leave me for her?"

"No! Hell no! Sage, sit down."

I plopped down at the table and watched as he pulled a chair next to mine. He sat down beside me and grabbed my hands.

"Sage, I don't want her. I've been over her for a while. The drinking and shit? That just became a habit, an addiction. It stopped being about her a long time ago. And…I love you. I don't know when it happened or how it happened, but I know I spoke the intention and it came true. I know my damn heart beats for you. I know you are my everything. You're my sunshine and my moon and my stars. I know I wake up in the morning thinking about you, go to sleep at night thinking about you. I wanna take care of you, undo the damage the men in the past did, fill you up with my babies, and will kill a motherfucker for putting their hands on you. I ain't going nowhere and neither are you. If I gotta rip my heart out my chest and hand it to you to prove that it's yours, I will."

"Neil?"

"Yeah?"

Through tears, I said, "I love you, too."

He grabbed me, holding me so tightly in his arms that I could barely breathe.

20

Neil

"Damn, that was easy," I muttered, as I picked up the remote and turned the TV on. I hadn't had one in a long time, years. When I was in my shit, I was barely home enough to watch TV, always at some bar or card game or something. At one point, I gambled both the TVs I did own away. I didn't care about TV, because I had my books and my Sage, but my Sage obviously wanted a TV, so I bought one.

I didn't have cable or a satellite yet, but I did have Wi-Fi and it was a Roku TV, so she could watch YouTube and Netflix and Hulu on it. She kept her eyes on that computer too damn much. She was going to mess her eyes up.

I was playing around with the TV when my phone rang. I didn't recognize the number.

"Hello?" I answered, eyes still on the TV.

"Neil?"

What the fuck?

I snatched the phone from my ear and stared at the screen, then put it back to my ear. "Emery? How'd you get my number?"

"From Jeremy."

I made a mental note to curse Jeremy's ass out. He was definitely up to something. "Look, I don't know what's going on, but I'm married, happily married, and the last time I checked, so were you."

"Yeah...I was, but Gala and I split about a year ago."

"Sorry to hear that."

"That's all you have to say?"

"What were you expecting? For me to bust out laughing? I'm sure that was hard for you and I'm sorry for that. I'd do anything to keep from losing my wife, so I get it."

"Oh, well...thank you, Neil."

"No problem, so...like I said, I'm a married man and—"

"I just need to talk to you. It's important."

"About what?"

"It'd be better if we did it in person."

"Not gonna happen."

"Why?"

"You really want me to keep repeating this shit? I'm married, *happily* married, and I'm not going to disrespect my wife by meeting up with my ex when I don't even know why the fuck I'm meeting up with you. So, you may as well just go ahead and tell me now."

"Neil, I really, *really* need to tell you this in person."

"You know what? I don't have time for this. When you're done playing games—"

"Fine! I wanted to talk to you about our daughter."

"Our what? The fuck are you talking about? I ain't got no kids."

"Yes, you do. A girl. She's seven and her name is Sophia. Gala took her from me, and I need your help getting her back."

Sage

He was mad at me, almost as mad as he was that night I went to the strip club. But this time, I didn't sneak off in the middle of the night without telling him. He knew I was at a client's house working. He just didn't know where the client's house was. But thanks to my car deciding not to start, he now knew.

He boosted it for me, and for some reason, it shocked me that he knew how to do that.

After he got it started, I said, "Thanks, baby. I hated to call you. I couldn't remember if you were going into the store or not today."

"It's all good. You done with your client?" His voice told me that he was trying to keep his cool, but I could see the anger in his eyes.

"Yeah," I replied.

"Good, I'ma follow you home."

"Okay."

When we finally made it home, I followed him inside, shut the door, and froze. "You got us a TV?!"

"Yep." He dropped his keys on the coffee table and dropped his body onto the sofa.

"Neil—"

"I don't understand you. I don't understand why you keep putting yourself in danger. I swear I passed a thousand little make-shift memorials on street corners in that neighborhood. What the fuck are you trying to pay, Sage?"

"Nothing...I just like my job, and a lot of my clients are my friends but they're not rich. They can't help where they live, Neil."

"Okay, is there a way you can do your job without risking your damn life, though?"

"Uh, if I had a space, yeah. I didn't think you'd want all those strangers in and out of here."

"I'd rather they come here than to get a call saying my wife got shot!"

"Okay, okay! You ain't gotta shout!"

"Yeah, I do, because you just don't seem to get it!"

"I do get it! And-and I'll start bringing the ones who live in the 'hood here. All right?"

"Good, because this shit is ridiculous," he muttered, rubbing his forehead. "We got any Tylenol? I got a fucking headache."

"No, I think all we got is Midol."

"Shit."

"Did I give you a headache? I'm sorry. I love youuuuuu," I sang, trying to lighten things. Neil was nothing if not intense as hell.

He looked up at me and shook his head, his eyes softer. "Nah, I just had a bad day, a really bad day. Look, I'm sorry for yelling and stuff, and I love you, too. I think I'ma go lay it down for a minute, see if that helps my head. Check the TV out. It's got a Roku built into it."

"Really?!" I bent over and kissed his forehead. "Thank you, Neil! You really didn't have to buy one, though."

"Naw, I didn't like you always looking at that computer screen. You were gonna mess your eyes up."

"Well, thank you again."

"You're welcome, baby. I just wanna make you happy, you know that, right? That's all I want, for you to be happy with me. Happy and safe."

"I *am* happy with you, Neil."

"Good. Enjoy your TV, baby."

"I will! Hey, wait."

As he stood to leave the room, he asked, "What?"

"Uh...you think maybe I could do something to help your headache?"

"Something like what?"

I grabbed the waist of his jogging pants and began pulling them down as I lowered myself to my knees. As I put my mouth on him, he said, "Shit! What headache?"

21

Neil

As I entered the house, Liberian music was filling the place, oozing from the stereo speakers in the living room, and there was an aroma in the air that made my stomach smile.

She was home.

She worked so much, it was rare that she beat me home, and when she did, it was like Christmas to me. I never thought I'd know what it felt like to come home to music and food and a wife. This was the life, for real.

When I stepped into the kitchen, I found her at the stove moving her hips to the music and stirring something. I eased up behind her, snaked my arms around her, moved her braids, and kissed her neck.

She turned her head and grinned at me. "Hey! You're home!"

Smiling, I said, "Yeah, I am."

Placing the spoon in the pot, she spun around and kissed me, and I took that moment to grasp her hips and move to the music with her. As we danced to a song I was now familiar with—Shine P's *Everybody Shaking*—I asked, "What you cooking, baby?"

Rotating her thick body, she shook her ass for me. "Rice with palava sauce. It's got fish in it, so I hope that's okay."

As she faced me again, lifted her arms, and danced into

mine, I said, "Yeah, I'm okay with that. It smells good as hell. What made you cook today?"

She shrugged. "I got finished with my one client early and decided to surprise you. Surprise!"

I chuckled. "I love your loud ass. You know that?"

"I love you, too!"

My phone rang in my pocket, and Sage said, "Go ahead and get that. Food'll be ready in a little bit."

"A'ight." Checking the screen, I frowned, watched Sage turn back to the stove, and then I headed to our bedroom, closing the door behind me. By then, I'd missed the call but called the number back.

"Hello. You're screening your calls?"

"What do you want, Emery?"

"You know what I want! Are you going to help me?"

I sighed. "Look, don't ever call me again. I'll call *you*."

"Neil, this is our child we're talking about. She is far more important than that little default wife of yours that you don't even want. I know you don't, because out of the tons of women you screwed when we were together, including me, none of us look anything like her. I know you were desperate, probably lonely, and she was all you thought you could get at the time, but I'm offering you a second chance, a chance to be a real family with me and Sophia."

Leaning against the bedroom door, I stared across the room at my reflection in the dresser mirror, and then I ended the call, shut my phone off, and joined my wife for dinner.

"Yeah, Nat! Go! Go! Go!" Everett thundered, up out of his seat, hands cupping his mouth. "Get it, Nat! Rawrrrr! Run like a lion!"

"Do lions run fast?" Bridgette asked.

"Who knows?" Jo answered.

Everett was acting like Nat had just hit the ball over the fence instead of barely tapping it off the tee, but she could run fast as hell, though.

"Yeah! There you go!" Everett screamed, once she made it to first base where she turned around and waved at him.

"I did it, Daddy!" she shouted.

"Good job, baby girl!" he yelled back, then his big ass finally sat down on the short bleachers and announced to all of us—me, Leland, Nolan, and our wives, along with Ella, and hell, even little Lena—that he taught her how to run like that.

"Daddy, you are doing the absolute most right now," Ella said.

"Uh, he wouldn't be your daddy if he didn't do the absolute most," Jo noted.

Ella laughed.

"Y'all need to stop hating. I do the same thing when I be cheering for Ella," Everett argued.

"Exactly!" Ella agreed through a giggle. "You even cheer when Lena poops."

"She poops like a big girl, though. Y'all some real haters," Everett mumbled.

"Whatever, Daddy," Ella said, bouncing Lena in her lap. She was getting big with all that sandy hair.

"So," Everett said, turning to me and lowering his voice, "things still good over in Venice?"

"Yeah, me and Sage are great," I said.

"Emery still popping up and shit?" Everett asked. "When I saw her at the club, I was like, 'The fuck?'"

I sighed. "Man, she on some real bullshit right now. Some shit I can't talk about out here. It's just...I really think she got a problem with me being happy."

"Yeah, that's what it looks like," Everett said.

"You good?" Nolan asked in a low voice, as Everett returned his attention to the game. He was the only person I'd told about this alleged daughter stuff. I didn't believe for a damn minute that she'd been hiding a kid from me all these

years, but if she had, that was totally and completely fucked
up.

I shrugged. "Shit…I don't know. It's just…"

"It's fucked up, but I'm on it. All right?"

I nodded.

"What y'all whispering about?" Sage asked, as she handed
me a little bag of popcorn and reclaimed her seat next to me
with a bag of Skittles in her hand.

"It took you that long, and this is all you got?" I answered
her question with a question.

"There was a line and it's a table, not a real concession
stand. Not much to choose from. So, what were y'all talking
about?"

"I was just telling Nolan about my birthday gift from you."

"Ohhhh." She grinned at me, tossing a piece of candy in her
mouth.

Nolan leaned forward to look at her. "Yeah, a complete set
of *Hidden Colors* DVDs and a *Wiz* DVD? You know your
husband, huh?"

"Yep. Three things he loves for sure: blackness, his mama,
and fuc—I mean, sex. Dang, I forgot it was kids out here."

"And you loud as hell, per usual," Bridgette pointed out.

"She can get as loud as she wants. The louder the better, if
you ask me," I said.

"Yeah! Run, Nat! Runnnn!!!!" Everett hollered, indicating
that Nat was back up to bat or had batted or was running the
bases, or something. Then his extra ass hopped up and ran
onto the field.

Jo shook her head. "I am so damn embarrassed."

I watched as Everett picked Nat up from second base and
hugged her. All the while, she giggled, and Ella said, "He
really needs help. He did me like that at an awards assembly
once. I'm scared to see what he does at my graduation next
year."

"Shoot, me too!" Jo said.

"Your daddy loves his girls, Ella," Leland stated, finally

taking his mouth off his wife's neck.

I looked up at Ella, who was now holding Lena *and* Little Leland. "Yep, we got the best daddy in the world."

Sage

"Stop laughing."

With my eyes closed, I said, "I can't, Neil. This is awkward. Awkward situations make me laugh."

"How is this awkward? Huh?"

"It's awkward, because I don't know what to do or where to look."

"Open your eyes, and look at me. I need to see them anyway."

I sighed, opened my eyes, and fixed them on him. He was so handsome, I swear he was painful to look at sometimes, and with his head in that pad, concentrating on his work, he was even more gorgeous.

With a creased brow, he looked up at me, his pencil moving as he stared at me. When I smiled, he asked, "What?"

"You really are a king, you know that?"

His pencil went still. "What?"

"You're a king, a beautiful king. So handsome, so fine, so sexy."

"Damn, what I do to make you say all that?"

"You treated—you *treat* me, like a queen."

"Because you *are* a queen, a gorgeous one. See?" He turned the sketch pad around to show me the drawing—me in my usual house clothes, shorts and a tank top, lying on the chaise on our patio, a headwrap on my head, my eyes closed.

"I thought you were drawing my eyes open."

"I like it better like this. What do you think?"

"I think you are ridiculously talented. She's beautiful."

He stood from his chair, setting the pad in the seat before joining me on the chaise. As he lay next to me, pulling me to him, he said. "She's you, baby."

"I know, but I think you made me look better than I really do."

"You really have no idea how beautiful you are, do you? I mean, you have no clue how luminous this brown skin is…" He dragged the back of his hand down my arm. "Or how your lips feel like clouds." He softly kissed me. "Or how I can see the past, present, and future in your eyes, how I can feel freedom when I'm inside you. You. Are. Beautiful. You are my world and my afterlife, the food of my soul, my thirst-quencher. You are my beginning, my end, and everything in between. My Oshun, my sangoma, my balm, my pain relief. You're my home, baby. My home."

After I blinked a few times, I said, "That was…poetic."

"I'm a poet."

"That's right. You are, my renaissance man." I kissed him and placed my hand on his cheek. "I love you, king."

"I love you, too, baby."

*****

"Sage, wake up."

"Uh…just…here." I lifted up on my knees and stuck my ass out. If he was gonna get it, that was the best I could do. I loved having sex with him, but a bitch was tired.

"Naw, baby, not that. Although I *am* tempted to say fuck it and climb in there behind you."

"I know you are. Freaky ass," I said into the pillow.

I heard him chuckle. "Baby, get up. I need to show you

something. And put on some clothes."

"Clothes? Since when did you start asking me to put clothes *on*?"

"Since I need you to come outside and see something. You know good and hell well I don't want nobody else seeing my titties and ass."

"*Your* titties and ass?"

"It ain't my titties and ass? Whose is it then?"

"I'm getting up."

"Yeah, you better."

Rubbing my eyes, I shuffled through the house in a pair of leggings and a sports bra, followed him out the front door, and screamed at the top of my lungs when I saw the white SUV sitting in the driveway.

"Is that mine?!" I shrieked.

"Yeah. All yours."

"Really, baby?!"

He nodded. "Really, baby."

I hurried over to it, ran my fingers over the hood, opened the door, and slid into the driver's seat. I craned my neck to get a look at the backseat. It was a Lexus NX with black interior, and it was beautiful!

Neil opened the passenger door and climbed in next to me.

"You got me a whole car?! I can't believe it! You got me a car! A *new* car!"

"Well, it's gently used, got like twenty thousand miles on it, but it's still under warranty."

"Can we afford this?"

"You don't check our account, do you?"

I shook my head. "I just been using the money in my old account."

"Yes, baby…we can afford it. I sold some tracks, ones Ev didn't use for the *Mrs. South* EP, to Ace Jace."

"Oh, I love his music!"

"Yeah, so anyway…we're good on money."

"Thank you, Neil. I love it!"

"I'm glad you do, and hey, when are you gonna start bringing your clients here? I don't care about you going to other folks' houses, but you gotta meet the hood ones here. I meant that when I said it before."

"I didn't know if you were serious about that or not. I mean, you sure you don't mind them coming here?"

"Yeah. Positive. Can't let nothing happen to you."

"You act like I'ma break or something. I've been out in these streets a long time, Neil."

"Yeah, well...I don't want that for you anymore. Plus, I'm your husband, and it's my job to look out for you. I love you."

"I love you, too."

We stared at each other for a couple of minutes, and then I reached over and tugged at the waist of his jogging pants.

"What you doing?" he asked.

"Pull 'em down," I replied.

His eyes darted around the outside of the vehicle, then settled on me. "You sure? Here? In the driveway?"

I nodded.

He lifted his butt and pulled his pants down. Just as I thought, he wasn't wearing any underwear. This man had an exquisite penis, and I'm not just saying that because I was crazy about him.

I licked my lips, leaned over the center console, took him into my mouth, and felt him flinch.

"Oh, we doing *this*? Shit! Okay, okay, okay..." he shouted, his voice filling the inside of the truck.

"Mmmmmmm," I hummed, as I pulled back, popping him out of my mouth. "Let the seat back."

"Huh? What? Let the...oh! Okay."

With his seat pushed back, I climbed over the console, kneeled on the floorboard in front of him, and resumed my work, bobbing my head up and down in his lap, slurping and sucking, feeling him grab the back of my head and gently push it, egging me on. His breathing grew louder and louder as I sucked and sucked, sliding my hand up and down his erection at the same time, and when he crested, I grabbed the sides of his stomach and accepted all he had to give, then I climbed up his body and kissed him, a kiss he returned with savagery, sucking on my tongue, holding my head so that I couldn't have ended the kiss if I wanted to.

When our mouths finally disconnected, he held my face in his hands and looked me in the eye. "When I was at the Sankofa center, the first few days were so hard, I wasn't sure if I'd live through it. It wasn't just the detoxing or the withdrawals—I'd been sneaking drinks when I was living with Everett—it was the counseling, the therapy sessions. It was hard having to face what I'd become head on. It was fucking terrifying to think about where I was headed if I didn't finish the program and get myself together. But hell, I knew what being fucked up was like. That didn't require work. Getting clean *did*. I started thinking about leaving, just saying forget it. And one night, after I'd been there for about a week, I had a dream. I dreamt that my mom was sitting on the bed next to me in my room at the center, and she told me not to give up and that she was proud of me for getting help. She also told me that if I held on, if I did what I needed to do to heal, I'd be given a reward. Now I know that reward is you, baby. You are everything I ever wanted, my dream come true."

I blinked a few times, fighting back tears. "You really mean all that, don't you?"

"Yes, baby…from the bottom of my heart."

"Neil, you saved me. I'm the one who won here. You saved me, *and* you fell in love with me. You know, I've had a crush on you for a while now, long before we got married."

"Yeah?"

"Yeah, but you never noticed me. You looked through me, just like everybody else does."

He frowned slightly as he gripped my chin. "Baby, I was too fucked up to notice anything good. Remember, I told you I couldn't see through the pain to recognize my blessings.

You're a blessing, but I had to heal in order to truly see you that day when we met to talk about the wedding. *I saw you.* I saw you for what you'd mean to me."

"Is that why you kissed me like you kissed me?"

"Naw, I kissed you like that because I *felt* you. As soon as my lips met yours, I felt your soul, and I knew you were my other half. I just had to get you to see it."

"I see it, Neil. I truly do."

"I'm so thankful you do."

22

Sage

"Girl, this is nice! Damn! You married up like a motherfucker. I mean, I knew he was Big South's brother, but shit! This house is the bomb! Nice furniture, and it smells so good! It's real clean, too. Can I get some water?" As Koko prattled on, I rolled my eyes and grabbed a bottle of water from the refrigerator. I knew she was throwing out hints for a tour, but that shit wasn't happening. I heard a long time ago from some old lady that you don't let folks see everything you got, and what I had was Neil McClain, who I'd left in our bed after fixing him up with some coochie. It was after nine at night, and I didn't expect him to get dressed and come meet her, and she damn sure wasn't getting a full tour on the off-chance Neil decided to stumble out of that pussy stupor I tried to put him in.

"Here you go," I said, handing Koko the water. "You can go ahead and have a seat. What you wearing tonight?"

"Oh!" She dug in her huge purse and pulled out a purple piece of super-skimpy lingerie. "This."

"Okay. Hmm. Let me go get my new eye shadow palette. I think those colors would work with this. Be right back."

I went to the room that was mine when I first moved in and grabbed one of my many makeup bags. When I made it back to the kitchen, Neil was sitting at the table across from Koko, and the two of them were in the middle of a conversation. I inspected him in his t-shirt and jogging pants and narrowed my eyes at him.

"I thought you were sleep," I said, as I unpacked the tools of my trade and sat so that Koko and I were face to face.

"Naw, baby. I didn't wanna miss seeing you in action for the first time."

"Ooo, he calls you baby?!" Koko gushed. "I love when men call their woman baby."

"Neil, you see me do my makeup all the time," I said, as I searched through my primer collection. "You've definitely seen me in action before."

"Not like this," he responded.

I left it alone. Koko was ogling him, but I knew she wouldn't get anywhere with him. As insecure as I still felt sometimes, I knew he loved me.

About an hour later, I was one hundred dollars richer — I gave her the loyal customer discount — and Koko was on her way to TNT to hit the pole.

"You're a magician," Neil said, as he watched me pack up my makeup.

"Why you say that?"

"Shit, you saw what you did. That girl was hurting before you fixed her up. This is what you do all the time? Transform people?"

"Neil, for real…why are you acting like I don't do my own makeup all the time?"

"Because you enhance your beauty. You still look like you when you're done. That girl looks like a different person!"

I shrugged. "I do what I can."

"You need an office or a salon. Do they call them salons where you do makeup?"

"Yeah, a salon or a studio or a beauty bar. Blac Chyna has a place where they do makeup."

"Well, you need one. I'ma make that happen soon."

"You don't have to do that, or are you already tired of folks coming here?"

"No, it's just that you deserve to have a legit place of business."

"Hmm, you know what I wanna do?" I said, slipping into his lap.

"What?"

"Go out. Let's hit *Second Ave*."

"It's ten."

"That's when grown folks go out."

"But I'm almost finished with the book I'm reading."

"Baby, I wanna say something, but I don't want you to get mad and divorce me."

He chuckled, wrapping an arm around me. "You ain't getting rid of me that easily. Say what you gotta say."

"I think...maybe feeding yourself all that heavy information helped you fall into that hole you were in. Well, that plus the not having sex thing. Anyway, your shit was off-balance. All learning and seriousness and no fun. I think that's why we work. I'm the opposite."

"Yeah, you are all fun, ain't you?"

"I try to be. So anyway, put the book down and take me out tonight. You owe me anyway. You didn't even have to non-alcoholic wine and dine me before we got married."

After he kissed me, he said, "Okay, baby."

Neil

She wrapped her arms around my neck and sang to me as we danced to Xavier Omär's *Afraid,* and I wondered if the words had ever rung true for her. If I hadn't been given the information that she was supposed to be my wife from Mother Erica and then received confirmation in my dreams, I would've been afraid to love her, afraid I'd mess things up. But as it was, I entered our marriage with confidence that everything would work out, because this thing between us was predetermined, predestined, and preordained.

I kissed her mid-verse, and she yelped into my mouth, then melted into me. Sage's body was so soft. I loved the feel of her in my arms.

We stayed out on the floor through a couple more songs, then headed back to our VIP seats.

"Hey, I'ma hit the restroom and go get some water. You want anything?" Sage asked, once we were on the couch.

"No, I'm good, baby. You know, you can drink alcohol if you want. It won't bother me," I said.

"My king isn't drinking, so neither am I. Anyway, you keep me high on you. I don't need to drink." She handed me her purse and cell phone, kissed me, and left.

All I could do was smile.

"What you up here grinning about?"

I watched as Nolan rounded the sofa and sat across from me.

"What you doing here? You not off making a movie or something?" I asked.

"Not tonight. Popped in here to make sure the place was still standing. The VIP room occupied?"

I shook my head. "Naw, you know Sage likes being out here in the middle of everything, so this is where we are."

"I know that's right. Keep her happy."

"Shit, that's what I plan on doing."

"That's your heart, huh?"

I looked up at my twin. "My *whole* heart. I need to be thanking you and Everett every day for asking me to marry her. But y'all still ain't shit."

Nolan threw his head back and laughed. "Look, I was tryna

keep my wife happy. You get it now, don't you?"

"Yeah, I get it. I'd wrestle a damn lion for her."

"Shit, I'd fight Mayweather for Bridgette."

"We some lucky motherfuckers, huh? Blessed."

He nodded. "We are most definitely blessed, little brother."

Sage's phone buzzed in my hand, and instinctively, I checked the screen. "What the fuck?" I said.

"What? Is that Emery's shady ass?"

"No. This is Sage's phone. Her punk-ass ex just texted her."

"What the nigga saying?"

I stared down at the phone, felt my damn heart speed up, and hopped up from the couch holding her purse and her phone.

As I rushed away from him toward the closest ladies' room, Nolan shouted, "Neil! Wait!"

Sage

"What the fuck is this?!"

I almost jumped out of my shoes at the sound of Neil's voice assaulting my ears the second I stepped out of the restroom. He was holding my phone up in my face, so close that I had to back up a little to focus on the screen, and when I saw the message, I dropped my eyes and sighed. "Baby —"

"I saw his other messages, too. This motherfucker been texting you this shit the whole time we been together?!"

"Baby, can we get out of this doorway? You know what? Let's just go," I said as calmly as I could.

"No, you wanted to go out, so we're out. Just explain this

shit to me, and we'll be good," Neil insisted.

"Uh, Neil, man. Maybe you should listen to her. This is personal business. Y'all don't need to hash it out here." That was Nolan, whom I'd just noticed standing behind Neil.

Neil seemed to think about it, his eyes still narrowed at me. Then he finally mumbled, "Let's go," and I followed his angry ass out of the club.

"I'm waiting," he said, eyebrows raised.

From my seat on the passenger side of my truck, I bit my bottom lip as I turned my attention to the text message emblazoned on my phone.

I see you still posting pictures on IG of you and that nigga you paid to marry your fat ass. Motherfucker must've been broke as hell to green card you.

"He sends this mess, and I just ignore him," I explained.

"Why haven't you blocked him?"

"I...I don't know?"

"You don't know why you been letting this nigga send you this shit for months on *my* watch?"

"It doesn't bother me. I don't care what he says. I think maybe if I blocked him, he'd think he was hurting me."

"Sage, I love the hell out of you, but that doesn't make sense."

The tears began to fall, and I didn't try to stop them. "Maybe...I think I look at those to remind myself that me and you aren't a dream."

"What?"

"It—I don't understand why you love me so much. The stuff he sends? That's what I'm used to getting from guys.

I'm—I was always a joke to them, something to do, someone to play with, and that's partially my fault, because I seemed to always pick assholes and then take shit off of them because...hell, I don't even know why I let them treat me like that. I guess I just didn't want to be alone. And look at me? I'm not what most people see as attractive and I know it." I sighed and sniffled. "Look. I-I'm not used to what me and you have. The way you treat me? It's hard for me to wrap my mind around it sometimes. I'm scared all the time that I'll wake up and realize this was just a dream."

"Baby..." he grabbed me and held me. "You don't know that my love is real?"

"In my heart, I do," I whimpered. "I *know* what we have is real, I do, but it's just hard to wrap my mind around it. I told you, I've liked you for a while. I've wanted you for a while. Besides my career, I've never gotten anything I really wanted before. Especially nothing like this. Not love."

I felt him sigh and wondered if he was just over me and my insecurities, but I couldn't help it. I knew he loved me. I didn't doubt that for a minute. I was just too messed up in the head to receive it properly. When I opened my mouth to try to explain that to him, he pressed his lips to my ear and began to speak.

"When Ev and Nolan came to me and told me about you, about your situation, I thought they were crazy. Yeah, I'd seen you hanging with Jo and Bridgette, but I didn't know you. To me, they were asking me to marry a complete stranger, and that shit wasn't happening. So I told them no and went about my business. Went to counseling—"

"With Mother Erica?" I asked.

"Yeah. I told her about you, about what Ev and Nolan asked me to do, and she advised me to do it."

"She did?"

"Yeah, she said you were my soul mate, the woman who was especially created for me, and I thought her ass was crazy, too, but I knew better. I trusted her not to steer me wrong. I just didn't understand. So, that night, I dreamed about you. You were sitting in your car, parked close to a bridge, a bridge I'd driven over before, and you were crying. I could...I could see the humiliation and hopelessness you felt. You were staring at that bridge and the water, and you kept saying that no one would care if you did it, if you jumped."

I stiffened in his arms.

"In that dream, I was there in the car with you, and I tried to touch you when you opened the car door. I tried to stop you. I kept telling you it'd be okay and that I would help you. I was begging you not to hurt yourself, and I remember it all felt so real. My heart ached for you like we were connected, like I was feeling your pain. It was kind of like the connection Nolan and I have. In the past, we sometimes shared experiences when we were nowhere near each other. I felt that same connection the first time I kissed you."

"I think I felt it, too. I just didn't know what it was. I'd never felt anything like it before."

"Me either, not that strongly. So, like I was saying, I tried to stop you, and then I screamed at you that I'd marry you and that I needed you, and the crazy thing is, I really felt like I needed you, and then you stopped, sat there for a minute looking around the car, and closed the door. That's when I woke up. I tried to go back to sleep, but every time I'd drift off, I'd see you in my dreams, feel your pain. And if it wasn't you, it was my mother telling me you needed me, that you were mine. The shit was exhausting. I couldn't get any peace or rest until I told Ev I'd marry you."

He kept holding me, and I let him, but I couldn't speak. I couldn't give him a response.

"I know this all sounds crazy. I know you probably don't believe—" he began, but I interrupted him.

"No...I know you're telling the truth. I'm just...I don't know what to say, because that actually happened, me being in my car looking at that bridge. I was trying to figure out how to get over the barriers, because I *was* going to jump. I *was* hopeless and humiliated, because I had tried one last time to get Gavin to help me. I tried everything...I begged him, literally fell on my knees and pleaded with him, and he still said no, and all I could think was what was the point? If someone who should've cared about me wouldn't help me, what was the use in living? I felt...worthless. I mean, I had my friends, but like you said, I couldn't see through the pain to recognize my blessings."

"Baby..."

"After Gavin rejected me *again*, I couldn't go back to Bridgette's. I felt so damn low, I actually slept in my car for a couple of days, finally made my way to that bridge, and I remember feeling like I wasn't alone and thinking that that should've scared me since it was the middle of the night, but it didn't. When I opened the car door, this overwhelming feeling that things would be okay hit me. I didn't know how they'd be okay, just that they would, and that made me close the door. That was the last night I spent in my car. When I talked to Bridgette, she told me she needed me to come home, because she and Jo had figured things out for me. Turns out you were what they figured out."

It was his turn to be silent.

"Neil?" I said softly. "Do you believe me?"

"Yeah, baby. I do. It's just...I think it's beautiful that we have this bond, that we had it before we ever knew we had it. I love you, Sage. I love you with my mind, body, and soul. I will always love you, no matter what, but you've got to believe that and stop doubting how I feel about you, stop doubting that what we have is real."

"What you just told me about that night at the bridge? I've never told anyone about that, not even Jo or Bridgette. There's no way you could've known. It doesn't make sense that you know. But you know. You saved me twice, three times with the club thing. I believe you love me. I believe you always will...and fuck Gavin and anyone else who tries to tear me down. Fuck 'em all."

"There you go, baby. There you go, and hey, when I tell you that you're beautiful, I mean it from the bottom of my heart. You are the most beautiful woman in the world. Hands down."

"Thank you, Neil. I believe you. I really do."

"Good, now block that motherfucker."

"Yes, sir."

23

Neil

I was laughing like I was at a comedy show. This Ryan dude was crazy! He'd actually run outside, and screamed, "You think you know a person and then they do this!" after his wife chose the obviously wrong group. This was what I needed to take my mind off this mess with Emery. She was still calling and texting me with that bullshit.

"Which would you choose?" I asked Sage, who was on the sofa next to me cracking up, too.

"I'm scared to say," she said.

"I know you playing! Come on, now! You would really pick Color Me Badd over Jodeci?! Please say it ain't so!"

"I mean…"

"Baby, for real?!" I shrieked.

"What Jodeci got that competes with *I Wanna Sex You Up*, Neil?"

"Shit, what Color Me Badd got besides *I Wanna Sex You Up*?"

"You can't answer a question with a question."

"Baby, are you serious? They probably got unreleased shit that's better than that! Hell, it's probably some stuff they threw away that sounds better than that song! K-Ci could sing while on the toilet taking a dump and it would sound better than *I Wanna Sex You Up!*"

"See, you can't name anything."

"You have got to be joking! *Forever My Lady, Come and Talk to Me, Stay, Lately.* I could go on."

"None of that is as good as *I Wanna Sex You Up.*"

I turned my head, looking around the room.

"What are you looking for?"

"Some cameras, Ashton Kutcher, anything to tell me I'm being *Punk'd*, because I know good and got-damn well you are not serious right now!"

"I *am* serious!"

My mouth fell open. "I gotta punish your ass for this. You know what? I'm cutting you off. No more Superdick for you."

She rolled her eyes. "Negro, please. You ain't went a night without diving in my coochie since we've been married. I don't believe you for a minute."

"Shit, I'm ready to dive in it right now."

"You're so damn silly. Hey, thanks for watching YouTube with me."

"No problem. I love watching YouTube now. They got all kinds of woke stuff on there. And anyway, I'm tryna make sure you ain't cyber-cheating on me."

"Through YouTube?"

"Yeah."

"Don't none of those men on YouTube call me their rib, probably because they can't see me through their cameras, but..."

"Oh, you like when I call you my rib?"

"Uh-huh...it makes me horny."

"Then I better do something about that."

*****

"You comfortable?" I asked. We were sitting side by side on the floor of the patio, facing the direction of the rising sun.

Sage nodded. "Yeah. I'm good."

"Okay, close your eyes and breathe naturally. Don't try to control it, just let it take its own rhythm."

"Okay."

"As you breathe, try not to think about anything and simply listen."

"To what?"

"Everything and nothing."

"Huh?"

"Just...be. Exist in stillness, and let the Creator talk to you. Try not to intentionally think about or listen for anything."

"Um, okay..."

Twenty minutes later, I opened my eyes and gently rubbed my wife's arm. "Baby..."

"Hmmm?" she hummed.

"It's time for the affirmations now."

With her eyes still closed, her "okay," came out on a sigh. Then her eyes popped open and she looked at me. "Wait, the what?"

"The affirmations. Stuff I tell myself every morning after I meditate. Positive stuff. Empowering declarations."

"Okay, show me," she said.

"All right." I closed my eyes and took a deep breath. "I am a king. I am strong. My strength comes from those who came before me. I am whole, healthy, and free. I will not conform to the ways of my enemies." I opened my eyes and dipped my head toward her. "Your turn."

"You learned to do that in rehab?" she asked.

"Uh-huh."

"What you said...you made it up?"

"Yeah, that was what was in my spirit."

"So I just make something up, too?"

"You say what's in your heart and soul, what you feel the

need to declare. What you're doing is speaking things that you want to be true about yourself aloud, whether you feel that they are true right now or not. Saying it helps you manifest it."

With uncertainty etched into her face, she gave me a little nod and closed her eyes. "Um…I am beautiful. I am whole. I am enough. Everything I do is successful. I…I can't fail. I *won't* fail to make my dreams come true." She released a breath, opened her eyes, and smiled. "How was that?"

"That was great, baby, and you know what? You done already manifested most of that, because you *are* beautiful, you *are* enough, and you have succeeded at making me love you."

"You always know the right things to say."

"I just say what's in my heart, baby."

"Thank you."

"No…thank *you*."

24

Sage

My tears wouldn't stop, and no matter how many times I was told everything would be okay, I just wasn't sure.

"Aaaayah! Wipe your tears! We'll be fine!" my papa soothed, rocking me in his arms. "*Get on Up...*"

I knew they would be fine, felt that in my soul. They were going to stay with one of my aunts and her husband in Nigeria for a while. They'd be with family. I, on the other hand, would have to live with my parents across the world when I was used to them being across town from me. What if I had a baby? How in the hell was I supposed to have a baby without my mother? And what would I do without being able to taste her cooking whenever the mood hit me? What if I just needed a hug from my daddy? My daddy gave the best hugs.

Those thoughts opened a new spring in my eyes and ushered in a fresh crop of tears. The US was my home. I was sure of that, and experiencing life with Neil showed me that staying was the right decision, the best decision for me. But the idea of being separated from my parents by ocean and land was truly heartbreaking and unfair as hell.

Fuck Forty-five and Forty-six and Forty-seven, too. Fuck the whole damn stupid-ass government.

I kissed my father's cheek, then released him, moving to my tearful mother as my sister fell into my father's arms. My sister and I were like day and night, nothing alike. And we had never been very close, because she always had a problem with my spontaneity and loudness, but in that moment, I could tell our hearts held identical pain.

I hugged my mother tightly, shut my eyes, said a silent prayer for her and my father's safety, and then backed away, feeling Neil's body against my back, his warm hands on my shoulders.

"You take care of her, Neil. Keep her happy," my mother said, her voice thick with emotion.

"That's my goal in life," he assured her. "Can't tell you how much I love your daughter."

"Oh, it shows. It shows," Ma said, wearing a weak smile.

A few more hugs and tears later, Neil and I were leaving the airport, and my parents were leaving the country.

Neil

With my eyes on the scenery outside my windshield, I said, "Yeah, I'm here now," into the phone.

"You sure you don't need any backup? I can be there in like thirty minutes," Nolan replied.

"Naw, man...I got this."

"If you say so. Don't get your ass arrested."

"Man, I ain't stupid."

"Again, if you say so."

I ended the call and waited, using the information the GOAT of connects had given me. I swear, Nolan knew everybody. No joke.

It took forever for him to finally come out of the building, but then again, I was early. The PI Nolan hooked me up with said dude took his lunch break at 12:30 every day he worked. He also provided me with his schedule and a picture of his car and license plates, so I knew his sorry ass was there, at a damn grocery store, a grocery store his parents owned but had his ass working as a bagger in. I guess that was all they trusted his dumb ass to do. According to the information I'd been given, this asshole couldn't even be bothered to finish high school and job-hopped like it was his profession.

I might've been a fuck-up on many levels, but this fool was just pathetic.

When I spotted him heading to his bright yellow Corvette, I jumped out of my truck and rushed the few feet to him. "Aye!" I yelled.

He looked up and around, finally settling his eyes on me, and the closer I got to him, the wider his eyes grew.

As he fumbled with the door handle, I stepped into his personal space. "You recognize me from the pictures my wife been posting of us?" I asked.

"Look, I don't want any trouble."

"Naw, man…that's exactly what you want, sending that bullshit to my rib. Looks to me like you were searching for the worst trouble, talking that shit about her paying me to marry her. With a pussy like hers? You must be fucking crazy. So let me make this clear to you, and I need you to *overstand* this shit: Sage is my wife, my motherfucking queen. It's my job to protect her honor, and if you even *consider* contacting her again, I'ma put my foot so far up your ass, it's gon' get lodged in your got-damn esophagus. You will be shitting my royal DNA for fucking decades! I do not play about her. Point blank, period. I will fuck you all the way up!" I didn't scream, kept my voice low and lethal.

"I thought she cheated on me, man! You two got married real quick after we broke up!" He had his hands raised like I was robbing him, and he'd backed up to the point that I thought he was about to climb on top of the car. "Shit, one day she was at my house sucking my dick, trying to get me to marry her, and a few days later, I'm seeing shit on Instagram about her wedding coming up in like two weeks! So I thought she paid you. The fuck was I supposed to think?! Then I found out you were Big South's brother, and I was just confused."

I can't lie. That shit hit me like a damn rock being dropped from an overpass, had my eyes all over the place. Now I understood how deep her desperation ran and why she felt hopeless enough to consider jumping off that bridge. When I lifted my eyes to that piece of shit again, I thought about him letting her suck his dick and then still refusing to marry her despite the fact that she was his woman and had lived with him.

He let her suck his dick and *still* didn't help her.

He fucking humiliated her. He was *still* humiliating her.

Yeah, I was going to have to beat his ass. There was no way I wouldn't, but as I balled my fist up and bowed back to fuck him up, someone grabbed my arm.

"Naw, bruh. Not today."

Motherfucking Nolan.

"Aye, man...let me go!" I said through clenched teeth.

"Nope," Nolan answered.

"Got damn, you two look alike!" this fool yelled.

"Nigga, I just saved your life. Leave!" Nolan advised, and Gavin's ho' ass jumped in that car and took off.

Shaking my head, I snatched away from Nolan and headed to my truck. "Man, you should've let me fuck him up!"

"And get your fresh-out-of-rehab ass arrested?" Nolan said.

"I been out for almost six months!"

"But you been married, what? Five months? You got a new wife, and you tryna get your ass locked up away from her?"

"He needs his ass kicked, Nole!"

"That's all you had to say. I'll take care of it just like I took care of that Emery situation. He won't know what hit him, and you won't have shit to do with it. At least not directly. How is it gon' look for you to kick that dude's ass, Neil?"

"Like it looked when Ev whooped Bugz's ass!"

"Yeah, well…you ain't got Ev's money, and you know you don't want him helping you any more than he already has!"

I leaned against my truck and muttered, "Shit."

"Yeah, so go home to your wife and chill. I got this."

Through a sigh, I said, "A'ight, man."

25

Sage

My eyes were stretched wide as I stood in the middle of the space. When I knew I was marrying Neil, there were a lot of things running around in my head, like how kind he was to help me when I needed it most and how at least he wasn't creepy. I was fine with sleeping in his guest room, had plans to keep hustling like I always do, save my money, and be ready to start life on my own once he divorced me, because this thing was supposed to be fake. But Neil was real. His love and concern for me was real. And this damn space he leased for my business was so real that I couldn't speak to even say "thank you" to him.

"Y-you like it?" he asked, as I stood in the middle of the floor and stared. "I know it's not huge, but the lighting is good, and you got lots of windows. It was a small art gallery before. And since it's in the same strip mall as my book store, I thought maybe we could have lunch together from time to time. And shit, this property is black-owned. You know me...I couldn't pass it up."

My eyes finally found my fine-ass, handsome-ass, sexy-ass, loving-ass husband. "I love it. I just...I don't know what to say...or how to thank you. I would give you some head, but I just did that last night, and that doesn't seem like a sufficient thank you anyway. I…I love you."

He pulled me into his arms and squeezed me to him. "I love you, too, baby. Now you have no excuse to be carrying your ass to the hood and them damn strip clubs."

"Neil, I stopped going to those places when you asked me to."

"I know, but just in case you feel like backsliding, you won't have a reason to. Plus, you'll be close to me in case you wanna take a break and thank me, if you know what I mean. Shit, you could thank me right now if you really want to. I ain't gonna stop you from showing me your gratitude."

"Oh, really? So you want me to put my mouth on you?"

He grinned down at me. "Helllllll, yeah."

I dropped to a squat, watched as he freed himself from his jeans and underwear, and I thanked the living hell out of him right there in a dark corner of my new makeup salon, and when I was done thanking him, he thanked me right back.

Neil

I was so proud of my wife; I couldn't stop smiling. After I handed her the lease I'd paid up, she quickly went to work furnishing the place, and had now been doing business in The Beatdown by Sage McClain for a solid week. The place looked good with its all-white decor — white chairs, including the two makeup chairs, white coffee table and couches in the waiting area, paintings of white flowers in gold frames. Sage really had a thing for the color white. I'd come home from the studio one evening to find that she'd bought a white bedding set for our bed. I liked it, and it did look better than the dark set I had on there.

So, the studio…Ev had me working on some tracks for a new rapper he was producing, the first act on his secret label, which he was going to reveal soon. He might have been retiring from rapping, but I knew better than to believe he'd ever stop working. That shit was in his DNA. That, and taking care of those he loved.

"Awwwwww!" the women in the packed waiting area said, as I stepped through the front doors of Sage's place with a bouquet of roses in hand.

Sage was busy working on a client, and when she turned to see what the commotion was about, nearly dropped her makeup brush. "Neil?! What are you doing here? Are those for me?"

As I leaned in to kiss her, I said, "Who else, baby?"

Another refrain of "awwwwws."

"Thank you, baby!" she squealed, as she hugged me.

"You're welcome," I said into her ear. "I'ma fuck you until you beg for mercy when you get home tonight."

"If you don't stop…" she whispered.

"Oh, you don't want me to do it?"

"Don't be stupid," she said under her breath, then raised her voice, and added, "Let me walk you out. I'll be right back, ladies."

Once we were outside the glass storefront of her place, she lifted on her toes, kissed me, and said, "Thank you for the flowers, but don't ever come up in my place of business when it's full of women wearing THOT clothes again."

"Jogging pants and a t-shirt is THOT clothes?" I asked, grinning hard.

"With a penis like yours? Yes. Love you, see you at home."

"Love you, too."

Sage

Superdick: *You still at work? When you coming home?*

Me: *When it's time for me to close. I ain't leaving and missing out on these walk-ins.*

Superdick: *I'm horny.*

Me: *I know, but I hooked you up before I left this morning. If you'd gone to your store, we could've gotten busy in your office.*

Superdick: *Shit, I'm leaving now. Call you when I get to my office.*

I rolled my eyes and relaxed in the makeup chair. Business was just as good as it'd always been. Shoot, even better since I was getting lots of walk-ins wanting to test me out and see what I had to offer. And my regular customers loved my spot. Having a salon was a lot easier than having to drive all over the place to work, so I was happy Neil had sense enough to lease the space for me.

The idea hit me as I sat doing nothing to call Jo and Bridgette, so I did.

"Hey, loud ass!" Bridgette answered.

"Hey, hooker! Call Jo and add her to this call," I replied.

"Okay, hold on."

Seconds later, Jo chirped, "Hey, wench!" into the phone.

After Bridgette informed her that I was on the line, I said, "I know we haven't talked much lately —"

"Yeah, we haven't, but Bridge and I know how it is being a newlywed. It's like these men wanna have sex nonstop once they put a ring on your finger. Not that I'm complaining, but that honeymoon UTI I got was a bitch," Jo said.

"Oh, I remember that! Shit, the way Neil be on me, I've been scared I'm gonna get one, too," I replied.

"So…y'all are still good, huh? He still giving you that good post-recovery, new year-new me dick?" Bridgette said.

"Girl, it's so good, I be wondering if I'm really me!"

"I know you do!" Bridgette shouted. "Same here!"

"Y'all, I love him so much, and I believe he loves me more."

"Sage, I am so happy for you two! I think you needed each other and didn't know it. Neil is so different since you two got together. I could see a difference in him just from when you moved in with him. It's like you're medicine for him. He's so happy," Jo said.

"And I've never seen you so happy and calm, with your wild ass," Bridgette observed.

"Girl, Neil got my ass on a leash. He's overprotective as hell!"

"Naw, it's been past time for you to stop that reckless shit you were doing. Ain't nothing wrong with hustling, but you take it to a new level. Ain't that much money to make in the world to be up in them smoky, musty-nut-smelling clubs," Bridgette said.

"Girl, and you remember that time I went with you to that one house to do that girl's makeup for her man's birthday party and that fight broke out? All those dudes pulled out guns and I was a half a second from peeing on myself!" Jo said.

I sighed. "I know, I know, and Neil is right. To be honest, it makes me feel special that he's so protective of me. It makes me love him even more."

"Aw, man! This worked out so well! Who knew you two would be made for each other?" Bridgette gushed.

"Neil did. He said he knew we were soul mates after Big South and Nolan asked him to marry me. And I've always liked him." I heard the door open and looked up to see a man entering my salon. "Hey, I just wanted to thank y'all for...shit, for everything. If it wasn't for you guys, we probably would've never gotten together. I gotta go. Duty calls."

After they said their goodbyes, I ended the call, hopped down from the chair, and approached the man who looked vaguely familiar to me.

"Hi! Welcome to The Beatdown! How can I help you?" I

greeted him.

He smiled down at me. "Hi, you don't remember me? I was at your wedding."

"I thought you looked familiar! You're one of Neil's friends!"

His eyes were locked with mine in a way that made me feel, I don't know, dirty, as he nodded, and said, "Yeah. We go waaaaay back."

"Cool! So, what can I do for you? You want to schedule a session for your wife or girlfriend?"

Another nod as his eyes raked over my body. "Uh-huh…"

"Okay, great! Will this be a surprise for her? Maybe a gift?"

"Uh-huh."

Before I could say another word, my phone rang. "Can you give me a sec?" I asked, and then turning my back to him, I answered my phone. I swear I could feel him looking at my booty. "Hey, baby. Guess who just walked in here? It's — hey, I didn't catch your name."

"Jeremy," the guy said, lifting his eyes from where they had, indeed, been glued to my ass to my face as I turned to look at him.

"Oh, right. Jeremy is here — "

The call dropped, and I kind of just stared at the phone for a second. As I started to resume my conversation with Jeremy, Neil burst through the front door.

"Neil?!" I shrieked. What the hell was going on? Was he right outside the door when he called?

"Yo, Jeremy! Get the fuck out of here!" Neil thundered.

"Damn, I was just talking to her. You still on that shit from back in the day?" Jeremy said, his hands raised. "You petty as hell, man!"

"What I'm on is the fact that if you don't get the fuck away from my wife, I'ma punch your ass into a coma. Get the fuck outta here, and do not speak to my wife again!"

"Damn! Okay! I'm gone! I'm gone! Hey, Mrs. McClain…ask

your husband about the little secret he's got with Emery, and when you're ready, I'm here for you, baby," Jeremy said, and then licked his lips, and added, "With your fine ass," as he backed out the door, and as I watched my husband chase after him, I wondered what the hell Jeremy was talking about.

26

Sage

"What the hell was that?" I asked, as Neil backed me into my salon. I'd been standing outside trying to figure out what the hell was going on.

He didn't answer me as he locked the door.

With my hands on my hips, I said, "Neil, why did you just chase your friend down the damn street?"

This time, he did answer me by grabbing my neck and pulling me into a savage-ass kiss that came close to making me forget what had just happened, but I made myself end the kiss, and with his hand still on my neck, I demanded, "Tell me what's going on!"

He yanked me to him, held me tightly, and uttered, "I just want my past to leave me the fuck alone and I...I don't want you to leave me," into my ear.

"Where the hell I'ma go? I gotta stay married to you and you know it."

"I mean...I don't want you to stop loving me."

"I won't. I *can't*. What is it? Did you cheat on me? You-you cheated on me with Emery?" My heart was racing in my chest. It wouldn't be the first time I got cheated on, but I knew this would feel different. This would devastate me.

"No! I'd never do that. I wouldn't cheat on you with anybody!"

"Then what is it, Neil?" I said into his chest.

He sighed, released me, and fell into the makeup chair. "I don't want you around him. I don't trust his ass."

"Okay, why?"

"Because he wants you, and he thinks I'm the same nigga I was back in the day."

"What does that mean? Wait, did y'all do a threesome with him or something? You had sex with him?!"

He stared at me.

"What?" I asked.

"Are you serious right now?"

"Well, I had to ask…"

"Sage, baby…I love the hell outta you, but don't ask me no shit like that again."

"What is it, then? What's going on?"

He fixed his eyes on the floor. "There was this one time when me and Emery were hanging with Jeremy and his girl at the time, and we all decided to start fucking in the same room, and Jeremy asked if we could swap women, and of course I was down, so we did. But that shit didn't feel right."

"This was before or after the lesbian threesome thing?"

"Before."

"Damn, you were nasty."

"I know, but like I said, it didn't feel right. I don't care about someone watching me get busy, so doing it in the same room was cool, but seeing her with another man fucked with my head, and afterwards, his ass kept asking to do it again, was always bringing it up. He enjoyed that shit too much. Hell, when Emery first told me she was leaving me, I thought it was for him. And now he's sniffing in behind you, but he can't have you!"

"I don't even want him! I thought he was hiring me to do someone's makeup or his makeup. Don't matter to me."

"You do dudes' makeup?"

I shrugged. "I have in the past. Money is money."

"Can't argue with that…"

"Look, Neil…it takes two to cheat, and I don't like light-skinned dudes or bald dudes, so if I was gonna cheat, it wouldn't be with him."

"That's supposed to make me feel better?"

"No, but this will. Why would I cheat on you when you make me come like I got a damn tsunami inside me? Who got a penis like yours with the skills you got? You think I scream in my daddy's voice like I do with you for every man? And last but not least, who besides you can love me like you do?"

"No-damn-body."

"Exactly. I love you, Neil Jason McClain. Forever. And I mean that."

He stood and hugged me again. "I love you even longer, and I mean *that*."

"Neil?"

"Yeah?"

"Why're you not freakier with me since that's what you're into? I mean, not the group stuff, but didn't you say you tied ole girl up? You gonna tie me up?"

His eyes got huge. "I thought me pulling your hair and eating your ass was freaky enough. You want me to tie you up?"

I shrugged. "Why not?"

"Damn, I love you."

Neil

"You good? You need anything else?" I asked her. Damn, she

was beautiful.

"I'm good, too full, but good. Thank you for bringing me here!" she answered, sipping on her water.

I shrugged. "No problem. I'm just tryna date you since you said I got off easy."

"You did! Didn't even have to work for the coochie."

I laughed. "Okay, I hear you, but I'm a hell of a husband, if I do say so myself."

"Yeah, you are. The best husband, and that's why I love you. I'ma give you so many babies."

I leaned forward, my eyes glued to her. "When?"

"When you want me to?"

"Six months ago."

"You're for real?"

"Yeah, baby. Once I truly knew you were my other half, I was ready. I told you my intentions."

"Yeah, but…my mama is gone. I don't think I can have a baby without her. Not yet."

"Well, when you're ready, I'll be more than ready. Until then, we'll just keep practicing."

She grinned. "Okay. Hey, you know what I wanna do?"

"What?"

"I want us to read a book together. Like our own little book club."

"You serious?"

"Yeah, but not none of that heavy shit. A novel, maybe. How about *Their Eyes Were Watching God*?"

"That *is* heavy, baby."

"But not as heavy as that stuff you read, and it's a love story."

"You've read it?"

"No, but it's Chocolate Shaker's favorite book. She was telling me about it the other day."

"Chocolate Shaker has good taste. Okay, let's do it. I know there's a copy at our store."

"Yay!" she squeaked, loud as ever. Sage was full of life, almost always happy, and that made *me* happy. She was like my own personal sunshine.

We stopped by my bookstore on the way home and picked up the book, and when we went to bed that night, I laid my head on her stomach and listened to her read chapter one until I fell asleep.

27

Neil

Everett's eyes were glued to the mixing board as he nodded his head to the instrumental I'd created for On-One, a rapper signed to his label. My eyes were fastened to my brother as I awaited his verdict.

As the music ended, Everett looked up at me and grinned. "Damn, Neil! You clowned with this one! And you wrote lyrics for it, too? I mean, this shit right here is lit:
'Girl, you're my all; fuck the money, fuck the fame.
If I'm standing in the picture, you're the film and the frame.
Shit feels so good, it brings tears to my eyes.
Fuck R. Kelly; when I'm between your thighs, I know I can fly.'"
After he recited that portion of the lyrics, he said, "That's crazy, man!"

I shrugged. "I'm a poet, man. It's just poetry."

"You been writing a lot of poetry lately?"

"Yeah, I have. Got me a new muse."

He raised his eyebrows. "The wife."

I nodded. "Yep."

"Good muse."

"The best muse."

"So, look…you must want a full-time job here at Due South Records or something, making music like this."

"Shit, the way you paying me? I definitely wouldn't mind."

He looked at me for a moment, then pulled out his phone. "I'ma shoot Wiggins an email, get him to contact my lawyer about drawing up a contract for you to be a staff writer."

"You serious, Ev? You're really bringing me onto your staff full time?" I asked, as I leaned forward.

"Yeah. You think you can handle that? I know you got the store to think about."

"I got a good manager, good employees. I just go there because I like working there sometimes, but I like making music more. And shit, the pay is much better."

"Good. I gotta rope your ass in before another label tries to get you."

I chuckled. "Yeah, right."

"Naw, man…that's what I never understood about you. You never realized just how talented you are. I can rap my ass off, got bars for days, but I can't make *music*. That's some real talent, Neil, and you got enough of it for ten men."

I lifted my hands, palms up. "It comes easy for me. This really ain't even work as far as I'm concerned."

"Because natural talent generally doesn't take much effort, but just like diamonds, it's valuable as hell. People can't buy that kind of talent, man. It's a blessing."

"Yeah, I guess you're right."

"Shit, I *know* I'm right."

I laughed. "So how is Wiggins working out?" Wiggins Westbrook was Everett's new assistant, an older black guy from England, I think. He was not the friendliest person in the world, but he was efficient as hell.

"Great. Shiiiidd, I think dude can read my mind half the time, and Jo ain't attracted to him at all, so it's a win."

"Ain't he gay anyway?"

"Exactly."

"Man, you know your wife ain't got eyes for nobody but you."

"And I'm tryna keep it that way. You and Sage still doing good, huh? Since she's musing you and shit."

I smiled. "Yeah. I can't thank you enough for that hook-up. I love that woman so much it drives me crazy."

"I know what that's like. It's the best feeling in the world, but it scares the shit outta you at first. It's like, you want to hold on to that feeling so bad you can't think of anything else."

"Yeah, man. For real, though. She's the main part of what I'm trying to keep together. Don't wanna go down that old road again…"

"Nah, you got this, man. You got it. You did the work, straightened yourself out, and you got you a good woman by your side. A good woman can keep you straight even when you wanna go left. I'm not worried about you fucking anything up. You see I ain't been on you or in your business."

"Thank God."

This time, Everett laughed. "Yeah, I know I was driving your ass."

"You were, but I get it. You were just tryna take care of me like you always have. I appreciate you, big brother. I really do."

"Hey, that's what I do."

"Yeah, it is. Like the wedding. I wanna pay you back."

"No, consider it a gift. But if you offer to pay Nole back for the pre-wedding stuff the women did, his ass ain't gonna turn you down."

"I already offered, and he already accepted it. Nole don't play about money."

Everett chuckled. "He ain't never played about money. So, you and Sage going to the premiere of Leland's company's first film? It's coming up soon."

"Yeah. Sage'll kill me if we miss it. She done already bought her dress and everything. She's hype than a mug."

"Good, good. I can't wait to see this movie."

"Me, either. Um, you heard the rumors about Esther and Bugz? I guess she and Dunn are…done?"

Everett shrugged. "Who knows? But I do know if that mess

is true, Bugz don't really want her, so I'm sure she's just something for him to do, and Esther? I guess she thinks she's hurting me by fucking people connected to me and Jo, but whatever. I got Ella out of that damn fuck fest, so I'm good. She can screw an orangutan for all I care."

"So, Esther didn't fight you on taking custody?"

He shook his head. "She ain't got a dog in that fight with the shit she's done that's public knowledge, and I honestly don't think she cares. Bugz has got money and he's probably spending it on her, so she won't miss the child support. Money is the bottom line with Esther, always has been. I wouldn't be surprised if her old ass pops up pregnant by Bugz."

"Man, I never understood why you ever fucked with her."

"Young and dumb. You know how it is."

"Yeah, I do."

*****

With my eyes closed and my head on my woman's stomach, I listened to her read from *Devil in a Blue Dress*, the second Sage and Neil McClain Book Club selection. I loved hearing her read and the way she'd do different voices and accents and shit. It was cute, and she really got into it. Hell, *I* really got into it.

She reached down and rubbed my head as she continued to read, and I closed my eyes, was almost asleep when she stopped, and said, "That's enough for tonight, I guess."

"Mmm," I replied. "That was good, baby. You want me to read next time? I know I ain't been pulling my weight with the reading."

"No, I like reading to you, and anyway, it's the least I can do with me grilling you about black consciousness stuff all the time."

"I like sharing my knowledge with you."

"And I like absorbing it."

"Good."

"Neil?"

"Yeah, baby?"

"I love you so much. Just thought you should know."

I looked up at her and smiled. "I love you too, but you know what else I love?"

"Uh, what?"

"When you sleep in a tank top and I wake up in the middle of the night and one or both of your titties is hanging out of your top."

"Wooooooow."

28

Neil

Sage glanced back at me. "You didn't have to come, baby. I promise I can handle this by myself, or I could've hired someone to help me."

I adjusted the box I was carrying and shook my head. "Naw, I wanna help. Didn't make sense for you to pay someone to assist you when I wasn't doing anything today. Plus, you said this was a black event? Shiiidddd, I'm in here, baby."

"I figured that was what this was really about."

"Yeah, an exhibition hall full of black folks sounds like a good time to me."

"Mm-hmm, but this is a beauty convention, so it's mostly black women, and I really don't appreciate you wearing that."

"I had this t-shirt made special for this occasion. You don't like it?"

She glanced back at me as we navigated the maze of booths. "I love the shirt, Neil, but those pants?"

I was wearing a red t-shirt with *The Beatdown by Sage McClain* printed on it in cursive black letters and figured red jogging pants would look good with it. And I was supposed to be working her booth with her, so I wanted to be comfortable.

I explained that to her, and in response, she rolled her eyes.

"Comfortable while showing folks *my* penis."

I gave her a lopsided grin. "Is that what's responsible for your attitude? Shit, Superdick likes to be comfortable, too. The more relaxed he is, the better he can work you."

We'd finally made it to her booth, and as she sat the bags she'd been carrying on the table, she said, "But I don't want other women looking at Superdick."

After setting my box on the table, I grabbed my wife and pulled her to me, kissing her neck and pressing my lips to her ear. "You want some Superdick before we start setting up? We can find a dark corner or a bathroom, and I can get rid of that attitude real quick."

She looked up at me with those almond eyes, grabbed the back of my head, and pulled it down to hers, kissing me while sliding her hand to my ass and squeezing it.

I was exactly a tenth of a second from screwing her right there on top of that table when someone cleared their throat and Sage snatched her body from mine.

"Sorry to interrupt, but I wanted to introduce myself. I'm Akeemah, one of the organizers," the short sister with a wild Afro said.

"Oh, hi! I'm Sage McClain," Sage said, shaking the woman's hand. She'd switched it up from braids to a short cut she'd dyed blond, and in a little pink dress and sandals, my baby looked good enough to eat showing those thick thighs. Damn, I loved her!

"And this is my husband, Neil," Sage added.

The woman offered me her hand, and as I shook it, she said, "So nice to meet you," while letting her eyes drag over my body. Then she turned back to Sage. "Um, I just wanted to introduce myself and tell you how happy we are to have you as a vendor."

Sage moved a little closer to me, her eyes on the hand Akeemah was still gripping. "Uh-huh...can my husband have his hand back now?"

"Oh!" Akeemah shrieked. "I forgot it was there. Well, let

me get back to work."

"Yeah, good idea," Sage muttered.

After Akeemah left, I said, "Baby—"

"I'ma have to deal with this shit all day. The curse of having a fine husband. Help me set everything up."

I chuckled as I started unpacking her equipment.

Sage

Things were hectic but fun with Neil by my side. I was doing discounted makeovers—fifty dollars for a basic beat with foundation, mascara, and lip gloss. One-fifty for a full-on glamour beat—and it seemed everybody who passed by wanted me to work my magic on them. Neil took the payments and helped me keep my tools organized, and I was glad to have his help even though those women were testing every ounce of my patience by ogling him and flirting with him. The man was fine, but really? I mean, I was convinced the line forming at my booth was more for him than me, but hell, money was money and I wasn't one to turn a dollar down.

When there was finally a lull, I collapsed into the chair my customers had been taking turns occupying and closed my eyes. "Whew!" I breathed.

"You good, baby? You gotta be tired; you been working nonstop since this thing started," Neil said, scooting his chair closer to mine.

"Yeah, I'm tired as hell, and my feet are killing me. I wore these shoes tryna be cute. Bad mistake."

He gave me a smile and patted his lap. "Let me see those

feet."

"Don't you need to scoot back some?"

"For your short-ass legs? No."

"I ain't that damn short, Neil."

"You're short as hell. You're the one who needed help climbing on a bar stool and shit."

"Why did I even tell you that? I was pre-drunk, Neil!"

"Whatever. You're short, and I love it. Now, let me see your feet."

I lifted my feet, placed them in his lap, and watched as he removed my sandals and began massaging my barking dogs. It felt so good that I threw my head back, and said, "Damn, that feels wonderful! Almost as wonderful as Superdick feels."

Neil chuckled. "Uh, thank you?"

With my head still hanging over the back of my shoulders, I said, "You're welcome. Hey, how much have we made so far?"

"Uh, almost seven thousand dollars."

"In four hours?!" I shrieked, lifting my head to look at him.

"Yeah, baby. You been running through these folks. Shit, you need to do stuff like this every weekend."

"For real, I do. Welp, I made that five hundred I paid for the booth back. Dang, that's crazy!"

"No, you're crazy talented, and fast."

I shrugged. "Been doing makeup since I was in high school. Once I match the foundation up good, the rest is easy."

"That don't look like you're doing makeup."

I looked up to see that that quip came from Bridgette. Jo was standing next to her, and Oba stood behind both of them.

"Girl, my husband is tryna save my feet. Y'all came to check things out?" I replied.

"Yep, and I need my face beat. Ev is taking me out to dinner later," Jo said. "Oh! I see you're using the *Mrs. South* lip glosses! Represent, sis!"

"You know it!" I hopped up and pointed to my chair.

"Come on, girl. Let me hook you up."

I was halfway done with her face when I said, "Damn, your nose is wider. The last time that happened, you were pregnant—Jo! Are you pregnant?!"

"What?!" Bridgette screamed. She was in Neil's chair while he went to find me something to eat.

"Huh?" Jo said, looking all crazy in the eyes.

"Bitch, are you knocked again?!" Bridgette yelled. Oba's eyes widened as he shifted on his feet where he stood right in front of the booth.

"Uh…yeah?"

"What?!" Bridgette and I shouted.

"When were you gonna tell us?!" I added.

Now people were slowing down or stopping, pointing fingers and cell phones at Jo. A couple of people tried to approach her, but Oba blocked them, pulled out his phone and typed something, and a few seconds later, Chink's huge ass was standing beside him. I guess our little commotion was drawing attention to her.

"Can y'all stop yelling? I just found out for sure yesterday. Four months."

Me and Bridgette pounced on her, hugging her and gushing our congratulations.

Neil returned to the booth with two trays in his hand, and after I gave him the good news, he said, "Congrats, sis-in-law. Damn, I'm jealous. I want a baby, but Sage ain't cooperating."

As I went back to work on Jo's face, I rolled my eyes. "We just got married, Neil."

"No, it's been eight months," he countered.

"Still too soon to be making babies, baby."

"Man, whatever. Since you got company, I'ma check some of the other booths out. I got us some vegan soul food."

"All right, thanks."

"He really wants a baby, huh?" Bridgette asked, after he left again.

"Yeah, but I really don't think I can do it right now. I'ma

need my mama to get through that," I responded.

"Girl, stop. You got us, and as bad as that man wants a baby, you know he's gonna be there for you," Jo said.

"Yeah, you're right. I'ma think about it," I said.

Neil was still AWOL when Jo and Bridgette finally left my booth, and his extended absence made me wonder if he was really mad about this baby stuff. So I texted him: *Where you at?*

Superdick: *Taking a dump. That damn chili dog I ate for breakfast fucked me up.*

Giggling, I replied: *Your vegan ass shouldn't have eaten it. I told you it didn't make sense for you to eat a chili dog that early in the morning, but you were on that, "my body told me to eat a chili dog" shit.*

Superdick: *I'm a pussytarian. Not a vegan. I told you that.*

Me: *Whatever. I thought you were mad at me or something.*

Superdick: *About what?*

Me: *The baby thing.*

Superdick: How I'ma be mad about that? If you ain't ready, you ain't ready.

Me: *You sure?*

Superdick: *Yeah.*

Me: *Okay. Hurry and come back. I miss you.*

Superdick: *Shit, I'm trying.*

Shaking my head, I shifted my attention to the action around me. There was a good turnout, and the place was noisy, but I liked the atmosphere, loved seeing all those fierce black women filling the space.

Superdick: *If I don't make it off this toilet, I want you to know I love you.*

Snickering, I replied: *Ummmmm, I love you too?*

"Sage McClain?"

I looked up and almost fell out of my chair, but instead, hopped up and with wide eyes, said, "4C Angie?!" Okay, so I yelled it, but I couldn't help it! I'd met her before, but that was one of those events where I had to stand in line just to say hello to her. Not this! Not *her* approaching *my* booth, because I didn't even have a booth at that event.

"Yes! Look, so many gorgeous women have been showing up at my booth telling me you did their makeup that I had to come meet you! Do you have a YouTube channel? How have I never heard of you?!"

"Uh, um...no. No YouTube channel. I just...I have a salon where I do makeup — The Beatdown, that's the name of my place, and I can't believe you're here talking to me! I mean, we met once at another expo, but I know you don't remember that because there were tons of folks in line to meet you that day. God, I love you so much! I'm a HUGE fan! OMG!!" I rambled.

"Shoot, I'm a fan of *your* work! You are so talented! I'm sorry I don't remember our first meeting, but I'm glad to get to *really* meet you now. Hey, Ryan and I will be in town for a few more days. Do you live here?"

I nodded. "Uh-huh."

"Let's get together, shoot a video. Let me give you my number..."

Minutes later, I was furiously texting a still-shitting Neil what had transpired between me and 4C Angie when I heard a voice say, "*The Beatdown by Sage McClain*...so you took his name, I see."

Emery.

Her eyes were on the banner that hung on the front of the table.

It was a beauty expo, so I should've expected her to be there since she was a hairdresser. But still...

Bitch.

Setting my phone down on the table amidst neatly situated brushes, palettes, primers, lipsticks, lip glosses, foundations, and highlighters, I said, "Well, he's my husband, so..."

Her eyes narrowed. I guess she didn't like that.

Good.

"About that. Can I speak to you candidly for a moment?"

"I have no idea what we could possibly have to talk about. My husband? I don't discuss him with people, so you can take your thirsty ass on."

"Thirsty?" she scoffed.

"Mm-hmm. You didn't want him, but now that you see he's happy with me, you wanna change teams again. Nope. Not happening. That man loves me, and I love him, so you can move right along. Bye."

"He might love you, but I know he loves our child more."

29

Neil

Sage was different when I made it back to her booth—quiet, almost sullen. Sure, she'd chat with the customers, still did a phenomenal job doing their makeup, would respond when I talked to her, but something just wasn't right, and I couldn't put my finger on what it was. Shit, she didn't even seem excited about the ten thousand dollars she made in one damn day. She'd said that was her first time vending at an event of that size as opposed to being an attendee, and as incredible as the results were, she kind of just shrugged when I gave her the total take after I added up the cash and credit card transactions.

The same applied to her when we got home. She was even quiet during sex, and later that night, I woke up to the sound of her crying.

"What's wrong?" I asked, pulling her to me.

She sniffled, burying her face in my chest. "You ever know you had to do something, that it was the right thing to do, but that your heart would break if you did it?"

"What are you talking about, baby?"

"Nothing. I just...I love you so much."

"You know I love you, too."

"I really do know that. I feel it. I feel your love for me every day. Thank you for loving me, Neil. You are so much more to me than you'll ever know."

"I feel the same way about you, baby."

"I want you to be a father. I know how important that is to you."

"It's important to me, but I can wait. I told you that. When you're ready, I'll be ready. Is that what you're upset about?"

"I just...I wanna do the right thing."

"You're doing the right thing by loving me. That's all I need from you. We ain't never got to have a baby. I just need *you*. Okay?"

She nodded and hugged me tightly.

I held her for a few minutes, then shifted her onto her back and rolled over on top of her, settling between her legs. Her eyes were glued to me as I kissed her, reaching between us and finding her clit. She flinched when I squeezed and rubbed it, gasped when I eased inside her, and whimpered as I loved her until we were both damn near boneless.

And then I fell into the sweetest sleep with her in my arms.

*****

The next couple of days she was still quiet, melancholy, and I didn't know what to do about it. I hadn't meant to make her feel pressured about the baby thing. Shit, I was fucking this thing up like I fucked everything else in my life up, and no matter how I tried to reassure her, my words didn't seem to penetrate.

Four days after the expo, she left early in the morning to film a makeup tutorial in her salon with her shero, 4C Angie. So to celebrate, I bought her dinner from her favorite soul food restaurant, lit some candles, put on some romantic Big

South music, and waited for her to come home where I was going to feed her and then show her my love with my whole damn body, but she didn't come home that night, or the next night.

I was about to lose my mind. I couldn't figure this shit out. It'd been three days since Sage left for work and didn't come home. She hadn't been to her salon, either. I knew that, because I'd been stalking the hell out of it. Jo and Bridgette hadn't heard from her or seen her. I'd even been to their houses, hoping maybe they were hiding her for some reason. I was acting so damn crazy, both Nolan and Everett separately threatened to have me committed but calmed down when they realized my damn wife was missing.

Missing.

Shit.

On the fourth day, Jo was finally able to get in touch with her and found out she was okay, but when she asked her where she was and why she'd disappeared on me, Sage told her she was doing what was best and that no one needed to know her location.

Doing what was best? Best for who? How was us being apart best for anybody?

I didn't understand what was going on. I was confused as hell, my fucking head hurt, and my heart felt like someone had shoved their hand into my chest and was tying that motherfucker up in knots. I needed my wife or I was going to fuck something up, do some crazy shit like climb out of my truck and walk in the liquor store I was sitting in front of and get pissy drunk.

Bourbon was my poison of choice. I loved it so much, I even drank bourbon-infused coffee when I was at my lowest. Bourbon was my best friend, my only friend for a time. Shit, if

I closed my eyes, I could smell it, taste it, let it warm me and numb me, because being numb was better than this. So I did that. I closed my eyes, imagined I had a bottle of Jim Bean or Evan Williams or Hahn. Imagined I was drowning my sorrows, diluting my pain, and washing away the fucking tears I was crying.

One bottle. That was all I needed. One bottle would knock my ass out quick since I'd been sober all these months. It would knock me out, make me forget how much I loved Sage, how much I missed her, how much I needed her.

Just as I said fuck it and decided to get me that one bottle, because getting drunk couldn't fuck me up any more than I already was without my damn rib, my phone rang. I snatched it off the passenger seat and checked the screen, hoping, *wishing* it was Sage, but it was Leland, whose calls I'd been ignoring like I'd been ignoring everyone else's calls. But something told me to pick it up. Leland was the one brother who always checked on me no matter how bad I was messing up.

"Hello?" I mumbled into the phone.

"Hey, man…you good?" he asked. I could hear Little Leland talking in the background. He was talking good to not even be three yet.

"No, I definitely ain't good, man."

"Yeah, I know. Ev told me about your wifey. Still haven't found her?"

"Naw, man. She don't wanna be found, and I wish I knew why because I miss the shit out of her."

"You love her for real, huh?"

"More than anything in this world, Leland. She's my everything."

"I know how that feels. She loves you, too. I can tell. She'll come back."

"I hope you're right. Hey, I'll call you later. Got something I need to take care of."

"A'ight. Be strong, man."

"I will."

I ended the call, and before I could put the phone down, it started ringing again. Nolan.

"Yeah?" I sighed into the phone.

"Hey…just checking on you."

"I'm…the same. Bridgette still ain't heard from Sage?"

"No, man, I'm sorry."

"It is what it is. Let me hit you back."

I hung up before he could reply, turned off my phone, and closed my eyes. Ten minutes passed before I opened the car door. A few seconds after that, I was walking the aisles of the liquor store.

30

Neil

"Neil? What are you doing here, son? It's the middle of the night." The foyer light framed her as she stood there in a caftan, a scarf covering her hair, sleep and concern in her eyes.

My response was to swallow back my fucking tears and lift the bottle in my hand. "She's gone."

Without a word, she let me in, led me to her office, and after I'd taken my usual seat, she sat down across from me and extended her hand. "You wanna give me that bottle, Neil?"

I blinked and shook my head. "Nah, I might need it."

Reclining in her chair, she asked, "And why might you need it?"

Fixing my eyes on that Sankofa painting, I sniffed and swiped my thumb across my bottom lip. "You lied to me."

"How so?" Mother Erica said in that even, calm voice of hers, and that pissed me off. My fucking life was unraveling, my mind was obviously messed up, and she was sitting there sounding like we were discussing the damn weather.

I tore my eyes from the painting and glued them to the bottle in my hand, motherfucking tears running down my face *again.* "You said she was my soul mate, my rib, and I fell in love with her. She was my Sankofa, or-or I was hers. I learned from my past so that she could be my future. She *was* my future, my world, my *everything*. I treasured her, took care of her like you're supposed to take care of a gift, because that's what she is or was — my gift! And now she's gone, and I don't know why or where. I don't know if she's safe! I can't…I can't take care of her like this! So do I need what's in this bottle? Hell yeah, I do! My life is just as fucked up as it's ever been, so what's the damn difference?! I knew this shit wouldn't work! I'm not supposed to be happy! I will never be happy!"

"But you *were* happy. I saw it."

"That just makes this shit worse. To be happy and then have it snatched away? I'd rather have never been happy!"

I heard footsteps but didn't look up when she assured someone that everything was okay. I knew it was probably her daughter, Annie, who helped her run the place. I did wipe my face, though.

Then she said to me, "Neil, I didn't lie to you, and you know I didn't. Your own ancestor confirmed who Sage is to you. You love her, connected with her before she became your wife. You saved her, remember? Through your dream, you saved her in her waking hours. She *is* your soul mate, and you *do* know where she is. If you could find her in a dream, what's stopping you from finding her now?"

That's when the light bulb in my head turned on. I set that bottle down and stood to my feet. "Yeah, I know where she is. Uh, Mother — "

"It's okay. You're upset. You wouldn't have used that tone or language with me otherwise."

I nodded, dropping my eyes to the bottle again. "I didn't drink. It's not even open."

Standing from her chair, she moved closer to me, resting a hand on my cheek. "Don't you think I know that? I know your strength, Neil. I always have, and now you know it, too. Go find your rib, son."

I nodded again, and then I left, powering my phone back on and ignoring the calls from my sisters-in-law and sister and brothers as I made my way to my wife.

31

$\mathcal{S}$age

Neil: *If you jump, I'm jumping right behind you.*

My head shot up as I looked around, trying to see if he was there. He wasn't.

Me: *Where are you?*

Him: *So you're still alive?*

Me: *Yes. And I'm not going to jump.*

Him: *Then why are you there?*

Before I could type out my response, headlights glared through my rear window, illuminating the inside of my truck where it sat on the little lot that people parked on to access the walking path that occupied one side of the bridge, the same lot I'd sat on months earlier when a similar sense of despair filled me. Closing my eyes, I sighed and popped them open when I heard him use his key fob to unlock the door. When he climbed in beside me, he didn't look at me, but fixed his eyes on his hands in his lap. His countenance was dim, and I could almost reach out and touch the pain emitting from him. What had I done? I was trying to do the right thing, but it appeared that I'd broken the love of my life in the process.

He wore black jogging pants and a black hoodie, smelled like remnants of his usual cologne, and as my eyes followed his gaze to his hands, I could see that he was rubbing his thumb over his wide gold wedding band, and that sight brought tears to my eyes, so I turned my head and re-affixed them to the bridge.

"Tell me what I did and how I can fix it, because I swear to God and Allah and Buddha and Olorun and Isis and all the rest of them that I can't live without you. *I can't*, baby." His voice was soft, shaky, heart-breaking.

I shook my head, stared at the steering wheel. "You didn't do anything. *I* did. I put you in a horrible position and I'm trying to fix it by releasing you, but I don't think I can. I've been sitting here trying to convince myself that I can be without you, but I can't. I just can't."

I felt his eyes on me as he said, "What position did you put me in? I married you willingly, fell in love with you purposely. You didn't make me do anything, Sage."

"But-but you want kids and—"

"Baby, I told you we ain't never got to have no kids. Is that why you left me? Where've you been sleeping? In here?"

"I haven't been sleeping, and what I'm tryna say is, I know about your daughter and how you want to be a family with her and your ex, but you feel obligated to stay with me."

"Who the fuck told you some shit like that?!"

"Em-Emery. You told her why you married me?"

"Hell, no! Emery told you that shit about that kid?!" he thundered, making me jump.

I turned my head to see fire in his eyes and creases in his forehead. "Yeah. So you didn't tell her why we got married? Why'd she say you felt obligated to stay with me, then?"

"Because she knows I always said if I got married, I was never getting a divorce. And she knows I meant it. I *still* mean it."

"Oh..."

"That motherfu—look, baby...I ain't got no got-damn daughter by her! This girl she's talking about is some cousin or something she and Gala took in. Gala's got the girl and Emery wants her back. She thinks if we get back together the judge will decide her home is more stable and award her custody. When she came to me claiming the girl was mine, I knew she had to be lying. I mean, I wasn't sure, but I knew I'd never been careless. Yeah, I was a sexual deviant, but not a dumb one. Shit, Ev schooled me a long time ago with him getting caught up with Esther. I've always believed raw sex is for wives. I ain't never been married to Emery's ass."

"But…how do you know the girl isn't hers, or yours, for sure? Accidents happen."

"Because I put Nole on the case. He got the info for me, and when I confronted her with it, her ass was dumbfounded. She thought I was the same pathetic-ass nigga who wanted her back so bad all those years, that I'd actually leave you because she said she had a kid by me, not ask for proof or do any research. Shit, I asked her who she thought was stupider, me or the judge? Wasn't nobody falling for that shit. Then she admitted that while she really did want custody of the little girl, what she wanted more than that was me."

I stared at him for a moment before asking, "And what did you say?"

He reached over and laid his hand on my cheek, making me finally release the tears I'd been holding back. "I told her that I'm happy, that I'm married to my soul mate, my other half, and that I intend to stay married to her until the day I die."

"And-and-and what did she say?"

"Some shit that don't matter."

"Something about me?"

"Something about me being a weak-ass drunk who she didn't want anyway."

"I'ma kick her ass," I whimpered.

He chuckled. "How about we just let Nolan get someone to do it like he did with that Gavin asshole?"

My mouth dropped open. "Is that why he posted that long-ass video on Facebook apologizing for all the wrong he's done? He apologized to me, his parents, his third-grade teacher, some kid he stole some candy from when he was ten…the shit was crazy! And he was wearing one of those halos like he had a spinal injury or something! Damn, what did they do to him?"

"Obviously, they fucked his hoe-ass up."

"Why didn't you tell me you had him beat up?! I woulda given you so much extra pussy and head had I known!"

"Shit, for real?"

"Yeah!"

"Damn…well, you know now so…"

I rolled my eyes.

"I didn't tell you because that was man shit. You didn't need to know."

"Why didn't you tell me about Emery and the fake kid? That wasn't man shit. I had to hear it from her at the expo when you were blowing up the public restroom."

"I didn't want to worry you, and I wasn't trying to disrupt my happy home. You were wildin' just from her popping up at the birthday party, remember? Plus, I knew she was lying. I guess she was so pissed about me rejecting her, she decided she'd try to ruin my marriage by telling you herself, but she didn't…did she?"

I wiped my face and shook my head. "No, but I really need to whoop her ass, and are you…it's not that I don't trust you, but you're positive that's not your child? I mean, it's okay if it is. We weren't together back then, so it's not like you cheated on me to make her."

"Hold on a second," he said, pulling out his phone, tapping the screen, and putting it on speaker.

A few rings later, I heard that stank-ass bitch groggily say, "Hello? Neil?"

"Yeah, it's me."

"Mmm, why are you calling so late? You finally came to your senses and left that fat woman who isn't even on your level?"

"Bitch! I'll tell you what's on his level! This fat pussy and fat ass he loves to eat!" I yelled.

Neil looked at me and held up his hand.

"Was that her?! You're still with her?!"

"Yes, you scrawny-ass ho', he is!" I screamed.

"Yeah, I'm still with her and I'ma need you to stay away from her and stop starting shit in my household with that fake kid lie. I don't give a damn if she leaves me; I'ma spend the rest of my life trying to win her back. I wouldn't get with you!"

"Yes, you *can* be persistent. Remember how you'd leave all those messages begging me to take you back?" the bitch said.

I had opened my mouth to call her a trifling ho' when Neil said, "Yeah, I remember that, but I ain't that man no more. A lot of shit has changed since then."

"Yeah, I heard you chased Jeremy away from her. What makes her so special when you let anyone fuck me?! Huh?! I did everything you ever asked me to and look how you treated me!"

Neil sighed. "Look, I know I was a messed-up dude when we were together and even after we broke up. I apologize for that. I am truly sorry for being so damn crazy back then with you, but I'ma need you to leave me and mine the hell alone."

"Whatever. You know you want me back. You *know* you do."

"Everything I want and need is inside the woman who has my last name. I'm good." He ended the call, and I stared at his phone.

"You still don't believe me?" he asked. "I got the proof at home. I can show you the stuff Nolan got for me."

"I believe you. I mean, the more I think about it, you want kids, so there's no way you wouldn't claim her if she was yours."

"Yeah, so can you not do this again? I know how we got together is about as unconventional as it can get, but we're in this, we love each other, and we want each other, right?"

I nodded. "Right."

"And we're adults. Hell, I'm pushing forty like a mug. We can talk to each other. Okay?"

"But you didn't tell me about the fake kid or you having Gavin beat up. You gotta be willing to talk, too. If I'd known when she came to me, things wouldn't have gone this way. I wouldn't have been caught off-guard like that."

"I know…I was wrong. I just didn't want to upset you about Emery and I didn't want you complicit in the Gavin thing, but I won't make those mistakes again."

"Me either. I shouldn't have run. I was just trying to free you of this obligation you made to me…"

"Sage, I am with you because you own my damn heart. That's it. Nothing more and nothing less."

"You own mine, too."

"And I'm so thankful for that. So, now that all that's taken care of, will you please follow me home?"

"I'll follow you anywhere."

With a smile, he leaned in and kissed me softly, then nodded toward the scenery outside the car — the sun rising, peeking over the bridge. "Grand rising, baby."

I returned his smile, and said, "Grand rising, king. And Neil?"

"Yeah, baby."

"I'ma need you to delete that bitch's number."

"Done."

32

Neil

"Why you in that phone so deep?" I asked, scooting closer to her in our booth.

"Posting on IG about that movie, because damn! I have never been so scared and turned on at the same time in my life! That movie was soooo good! And the title? *Wolfe*? It definitely fit, because he was a savage with that coochie! Now I wanna read the book!"

"Yeah, it was a great movie. Score could've been better, though. Man, if I'd had my shit together when Leland and his partners made that movie, I could've composed some crazy music for it."

"Like what you're working on for Nolan's and Big South's next movie? That music is ridiculously good!"

"Thank you, baby, but I'ma need you to get out of your phone and pay attention to your husband."

She set her phone down and smiled at me. "You jealous?"

"Yep."

After she kissed me, she said, "Big baby." Her eyes surveyed the club, and then she added, "Where's everybody else? I mean, this place is packed, but I thought this was supposed to be where the premiere's after-party was at. I don't see your brothers or your sister or Bridgette or Jo or —"

"That's because they're at a different club."

She turned to face me, a slight frown on her face. "Then what are we doing here?"

"Fulfilling your fantasy."

"Huh?"

I loosened my tie and pushed the table back a little. "Come here, baby. Sit on my lap."

"What? Why?"

"Because I'm about to fuck the shit outta you in this club."

"Ohhhhhhh! That's why we're back here in this dark corner?"

"Yeah, baby. Come here."

Her eyes were wild as she pulled her red dress up and climbed into my lap, straddling me.

I kissed her as I pulled my tie off. "Let me see your hands."

Wearing an unsure expression, she presented her hands to me and I clasped them between mine, kissing each finger and then binding her wrists with my tie. Her eyes rose from her hands to my eyes, wide with excitement. She didn't say a word as I reached between us, sliding her panties to the side and finding my way to her treasure, easing my fingers inside to stroke that special spot a couple of inches inside of her. I massaged that spot, rubbing her clit with my thumb as she threw her head back and moaned loudly, but I was sure no one could hear her over the speakers blasting Kodak Black's ZEZE.

"Oooooo, baby!" she groaned, lowering her head to kiss me.

I kept working her spot, rubbing her clit, and tasting her mouth until she started trembling, tearing her mouth away from mine as tears ran down her cheeks. She grabbed my shirt collar with her restricted hands, breathing harshly with her eyes on me, her eyebrows knitted together.

"Shhhhit!" she whimpered, as she finally came down from her orgasm.

"Lift up a little, baby," I said, licking my lips and reaching between us to unfasten my belt and unbutton my pants. A second or so later, she was sinking down on me with a gasp, and I was moaning at the slippery hotness that surrounded me. I gripped her ass as she slid up and down me, her hands on my chest.

"You feel that, baby? Huh? You feel that?" I murmured, clutching her face and kissing her.

"Oooooo, shit! I feel it!" she yelled into my mouth.

I grabbed her freshly-braided hair, yanking her head back and sucking on her neck as she rode me to the rhythm of Drake's *Don't Matter to Me*, her face in a beautiful contortion as another orgasm seized her. I could feel eyes on us in the dimness, almost hear their thoughts, and that shit turned me completely on. Made me thrust upward and squeeze her ass in my hands. And when I finally hit my peak, I grabbed her, holding onto her like she'd fly away if I didn't, and as I emptied inside her, I damn near shouted, "I love you so fucking much!"

"I love you, too!!!!"

33

Sage

1 year later...

"Okay, first of all, I wanna say how proud I am of my baby girl, Ella, for graduating with honors. This was my last summer with you before you go off to college. You'll be leaving soon, and I don't know how to feel. Seems like time just flew by." Big South grasped the back of his chair and shook his head as Ella jumped up from her seat and wrapped her arms around him.

"Oh, Daddy," she whimpered.

He hugged her to him as he continued his speech. "Like I was saying, I'm proud of you, baby girl. Proud of your academic achievements, proud of what a great big sister you are to Nat and Lena and Little Everett. Jo says all the time that she doesn't know what she's gonna do when you leave us."

"For real?!" Ella squeaked into Big South's chest.

"Yes, for real," Jo said, her voice trembling.

At that, Ella moved from her father to Jo sitting right next to him, bending over to hug her. At the same time, Nat left her chair, tugging on Big South's pant leg.

"Come on, Nat-Nat," he said, picking her up. "And for the

second reason for this celebration. Nat is officially a McClain! Thanks for all your help getting Bugz on board with this adoption, Nole!"

As everyone cheered, Nolan nodded. "You know I got you."

"So, I ain't tryna be up here all day. I mean, I ain't Nolan," Big South quipped, making Bridgette spit out her water and laugh while Nolan very conspicuously threw up his middle finger at his big brother. "I just wanna say that I'm proud of our family, proud of how it's growing. Leland and Kim got another one on the way. Congrats, y'all!"

"I don't know why I let him talk me into this," Kim muttered, as she rubbed her huge stomach.

Leland leaned in and kissed her. "Because you love me."

"Yeah, I do," she replied, grinning.

"Nole and Bridgette still on that no kids bull."

"Much as we babysit when we're in town, you oughta be glad we aren't having kids," Bridgette said.

"True, true," Big South agreed.

Just then, Neil rushed from inside Big South's and Jo's house to the backyard, our three-month-old son in his arms.

As he plopped down in the seat next to mine, I softly asked, "Everything okay? I see you changed his clothes."

"His little ass had a blowout."

"He got a stomach just like his daddy."

"Stop hating."

"How I'ma hate on you having bubble guts?"

"Because that's what haters do, hate on any and everything. Y'all okay? She don't need to be changed?"

"Unlike her brother, she didn't inherit your bad guts, so she's fine."

"...my head staff writer over there, who ducked out on my speech," Big South said.

"Man, you been up there talking for three days. Always calling me long-winded," Nolan shouted.

"Shut up, Nole!" Big South shot back.

"Daddy duties, man," Neil explained.

"Well, I'm proud of you, too. Got your rib — *the YouTube star* — and your twins, you're making good music…you're doing it, man," Big South continued.

"Gotta do it for my family."

"And Kat. Tommy, I still owe you an ass-whooping for sneaking around with my little sister, but — "

"Ass!" Nat screamed, her little arms still around Big South's neck.

Everyone sitting around the tables occupying the backyard laughed, and poor Big South looked like he wanted to run as far away from there as possible.

"Don't say that, Nat," he begged.

"Dang, she still copying you?" Leland asked.

Jo just shook her head as she covered their little boy's ears. That boy was so much like his daddy, it was scary!

"Uh, anyway…" Big South continued. "I'm still tryna figure out how y'all two got together."

"Maybe we'll tell our story one day," Kat said, leaning in to kiss her man.

"Well, I can see you're keeping my sister happy, so I guess I'll let you slide, Tommy."

"Let him slide? Kat's mean butt be done tore you up for messing with him!" Aunt Ever said, chuckling as her husband threw his head back and laughed. Little Lena, who was sitting in her lap, even giggled.

"Tick, that big negro of Kat's be done knocked you into next week. You ain't got no choice but to let him slide!" Uncle Lee Chester shouted from his post at the grill. "By the way, ribs done! Pineapples, too!"

Whether Big South was done with his speech or not, there was a mass exodus from the area scattered with tables and chairs to the grill.

"Kim, you need to load up on those pineapples," Leland called after his wife, as his little boy tagged along behind her.

"Here, take Oya, too, so I can go make us some plates," I

said to Neil, but Teetee Bridgette swooped in and took her from me.

"I got her. OMG, she and Olu are getting so big!" she gushed, peppering my baby girl's cheeks with kisses.

"Hell, they were born big. Remember?" I said.

"True. I don't know how you carried all that around. Girl, you are the truth!"

"Yeah, she is," Neil agreed. "Nothing but the truth."

As I stood in line with our plates, I let my eyes peruse the crowd of family in the huge yard, thinking how this was so different from how I felt back when I didn't know where to turn or what to do, when my future was uncertain and my heart was broken. Never in a million years did I think I'd be living this life, but now, it felt like I'd always been married, always been a mother, always been a part of this beautiful family, and always been so…happy. I was so blessed even with my parents being far away from me. We kept in touch, I knew they were fine, and as soon as I was eligible to go from a green card-holder to a citizen, I was going to get a passport and go visit them. But in every way that counted, this was my family, too, and they helped me, accepted me. And my man? Damn, I loved me some him.

And he loved the hell out of Sage Marjoram Moniba-McClain. That, I knew without a single doubt.

Neil

"Who is that dancing with Uncle Lee Chester?" Leland asked.

"Hell if I know. Why? You thinking about cheating on Kim with her?" Everett asked.

"You can fuck yourself right now. I don't mind. Go ahead.

Fuck yourself real good, Ev," Leland replied.

"For real. She's what? Sixty, seventy? I know your ass is drooling."

"Suck a dick, Ev. Suck a mean dick."

"I ain't gonna lie. She's in shape, been keeping her balance good with Unc hunching all over her," Nolan said.

"Did he bring her?" I asked.

"What y'all McClain brothers over here talking about?" Bridgette questioned, as she approached the table the four of us were sitting at.

"That chick with Uncle Lee," Nolan said.

"That's how you refer to your aunt?"

"Our aunt?!" all four of us damn near shouted.

"Which aunt is she?" Everett asked.

"Lou!" Bridgette informed us.

"That's Aunt Lou? You're shitting me!" Nolan said.

As she slid into Nolan's lap, Bridgette explained, "No, I introduced myself to her and she said she was Lee Chester's wife, Lou—actually, she said her name was Lou Bertha...poor woman. Then she told me she was Lunch Meat's mama, and I was like, why didn't I know this? I didn't know Unc had kids. I wasn't sure who Lunch Meat's big ass belonged to. And he's so quiet, who woulda known he was Uncle Lee's?"

"I didn't tell you? My bad. Unc got an outside kid, too, but we don't talk about that," Nolan said. "So that's Aunt Lou, huh?"

"Wait, you don't know her? You don't know your aunt when you see her?"

"We ain't never seen her. I mean, I know I haven't," I told her.

"What?!" Bridgette shrieked. And as the rest of our wives joined us, all holding a baby—Kim had my Olu, Jo had Little Ev, and Sage had my Oya while Little Leland, Nat, Lena, and Kat's Little Randy ran around the yard chasing Ella—she added, "Are you serious?"

Once my brothers confirmed that they had never seen her either, Everett called Kat over to us and asked her if she knew who the woman was, to which Kat replied, "Shit, I don't know." Her mouth fell open when Bridgette told her it was our Aunt Lou.

Sage handed Oya to me and then stood behind me. "She's cute, though. And in shape. You see how she's backing it up on Uncle Lee? She's been backing it up for a minute, too."

"Hey, Nolan! This what I was talking about! See how I'm doing this? Bam! Bam! Bam!" With each bam, he thrusted his hips, popping Aunt Lou in the ass with his groin. "This how you stand up in it!"

All you could hear was snickering as Nolan shook his head, and said, "Yeah, I see you, Unc."

"And later on tonight, I'm gon' put some ribs on her ass and go to town! Ha-haaaa!"

"Someone should round the kids up and take them inside before they're scarred for life," Everett said.

"Take Little Ev, I'll get 'em," Jo offered. "Ella can help me."

"Just don't put no greens on me! Last time, that green juice got everywhere. Stained up my sheets and the damn mattress!" the trim older woman said. Aunt Lou wasn't bad-looking in her red wig, heavy makeup, and purple dress. Those green shoes didn't match, but I guess Unc liked it.

"Now, look. I told you I wasn't gonna do greens again, shit!" Uncle Lee shouted.

"What time is it? They got MeTV here? I can't miss *Columbo*." That was Aunt Lou.

"You done seen every episode! I swear I shoulda left yo' ass in Texas!"

"That woulda been fine with me! You the one who wanted me to come, kept fussing about me staying in the house, talking 'bout we could get freaky in your nephew's mansion!"

"The fuck?" Everett mumbled.

"Woman, you ain't worth the spit it takes to cuss you!"

"Yes, I am!"

"And I still ain't got over you breaking my damn TV! My *color* TV! Shit! Got a call! What-up-there-now?! Earl? Yeah…what? Ha-haaa!! I wish I was there to kick some spades ass, but I'm in LA at my nephew's house…it's two rich ones…not my Kimmy's husband, the rapper."

"His what?! That's it. I *gotta* kick his ass," Leland said, but Kim plopped down in his lap and started kissing him before he could make a move.

"Yeah!" Uncle Lee continued. "Okay, talk to you later." He tapped that Bluetooth button and returned his attention to his wife, who'd just been standing next to him watching him talk. "Now, where was I?"

"You was talking shit about that old-ass TV!" Aunt Lou shouted.

"It was only twenty years old, woman! Shit!"

As they continued to argue, and my family watched them like they were a damn movie, I first kissed my baby girl, then my wife, looked around at my family, then closed my eyes and smiled. Life was good.

Life was real good.

Epilogue

Sage

10 months earlier...
The future...

This was my favorite part of the day, a part that had become as routine for me as it was for Neil. With the warmth of the newly-risen sun on my face, I sat on the patio floor, eyes closed, absorbing the stillness, quiet, and peace of this rising. The gentle sounds of nature provided the melody of the morning's soundtrack. The calm beating of my heart and the rhythm of my breathing were the cadence. The only problem was that my mind wasn't empty but racing with thoughts, exciting thoughts about our future, our hope, and our love.

All of that made me smile and sigh. And to think, I almost let that Emery ho' mess up the best thing that ever happened to me — hands down.

The heat of Neil's hand capped my bare shoulder. Slowly, I peeled my eyes open to look at him. So handsome and sexy and passionate and loving and mine.

All mine and mine alone...for now.

"Time for the affirmations, baby," he said softly, his lush lashes waving at me as he blinked his eyes.

"Okay. Can I go first?" I replied.

Surprise quickly registered on his face. "Yeah, sure. Go ahead."

With a quickened pulse, I took a deep breath, and instead of facing the sun as I usually did, I fixed my eyes on him. "I am beautiful. I am loved by the best husband in the world. My life is just as it should be, and the baby I'm carrying is healthy and strong and smart just like his or her daddy, a warrior with his confidence and self-awareness and loving heart. Our baby—"

"Wait, you said the baby you're carrying, as in already carrying, or are you trying to manifest a baby?"

"No, what I'm saying is we've already manifested the hell out of a baby. I'm pregnant!"

"But...we ain't even been trying that long. My sperm is stronger than a motherfucker!"

Before I could agree, he grabbed the sides of my face and kissed me hard, then snatched me into his arms, then let me go. "Shit, I ain't mean to be so rough, but you're having my baby? For real?"

"Yes! For real!"

"I'm so damn happy, baby! I don't even need to do my affirmations today. I got everything I want!" He leaned in and kissed me gently this time, then added, "You sure it's just one?"

"No, haven't been to the doctor yet, and I think it's probably too early to tell...I guess. Anyway, I want you to go with me. You think it could be twins? What the hell am I gonna do with twins?!"

"Come on, now. I got you. You know that."

I fell against him and he wrapped his arms around me. "Yeah, I definitely know that."

"I'm so happy, baby. Everything is...it's the way it should be. You know?"

"It really is."

We sat there holding each other until the ringing of a cell phone floated from inside the house through the open patio doors.

"That's mine. Forgot to turn it off. Glad whoever it is decided to call after we finished meditating," he said.

"Well, come on. You can answer it while I fix us some

breakfast. I'm starving."

Neil

I'd missed the call by the time we made it in the house. As Sage headed to the kitchen, I made a detour to our bedroom and grabbed my phone, had stepped into the kitchen when I informed her that the call was from Uncle Lee Chester.

"You gonna call him back?" she asked.

"It's early enough that he might actually want something, so yeah."

After I tapped the missed call notification to call him back, I set the phone on the table and activated the speakerphone while I slid into one of the chairs. After a couple of rings, his voice boomed from the phone's speakers.

"Neil!"

"What up, Unc? You called?"

"Yeah! How you and Sadie doing?"

Sage covered her mouth as she giggled.

"We good, Unc. Real good."

"Good, Nephew. Look, I was calling because I thought about something. You know, I been helping Nolan with his wife and shit, giving him advice 'cause he ain't used to black womens."

"Yeah, I know. He appreciates it, too. You should call him more often, give him more advice. He wanted to tell you that, but you know...he was too proud to."

Sage turned and looked at me with wide eyes, mouthing, "You are wrong for that."

I shrugged in response, giving her a lopsided grin.

"Sho' nuff?" Unc said.

"Yeah!" I replied.

"Thanks for letting me know! Matter of fact, I'ma call him after I hang up with you. But anyway, I thought, 'Now Lee, it ain't right to help one twin and not the other.'"

"Ha!" Sage said, then covered her mouth.

With stretched eyes, I fell back in my seat. "Uh, Unc...I don't need—"

"I know you always messed with black girls, but it's been awhile since you had a girlfriend and now you got a wife. I know you tryna keep her 'cause she all African and shit. So listen here. What you know about the click?"

"The click?" I asked.

"The click! The pearl tongue! The little man in the boat! What you know about that?"

"You talking about the clit, Unc?"

"Yeah! That's what I said! The click!"

By then, Sage was doubled over laughing.

"Unc, I know plenty about the clit—" I tried.

"Let me tell you what you gotta do with that sum-bitch. You gotta work it! You gotta knock the man out the boat! Neil, do you like eating at the breakfast buffet?"

"What?" I asked, looking up to see Sage wiping tears.

"Damn, boy! I gotta teach you everything? Do you like eating at the breakfast buffet, going down the town, stepping down the stairs, doing a seventy-nine?!"

"Unc, are you talking about eating pussy?"

"Uh-huh. You know how to do that?"

"Yeah, I do—"

"This is how you do it..."

As Uncle Lee went about the business of giving me the most inaccurate and disturbing lesson of my life, Sage moved behind me and wrapped her arms around my neck, then she pressed her lips to my ear, and whispered, "I love you and the whole crazy-ass McClain family. You know that?"

I smiled, and whispered back, "We love you, too, but I love you most."

"Mmmm…" she sighed. "Asé, king."
"So it is, baby. So it is."

A southern girl at heart, Alexandria House has an affinity for a good banana pudding, Neo Soul music, and tall black men in suits. When this fashionista is not shopping, she's writing steamy stories about real black love.

Connect with Alexandria!
Email: msalexhouse@gmail.com
Website: http://www.msalexhouse.com/
Newsletter: http://eepurl.com/cOUVg5
Blog: http://msalexhouse.blogspot.com/
Facebook: Alexandria House
Instagram: @msalexhouse
Twitter: @mzalexhouse

Also by Alexandria House:

The McClain Brothers Series:
Let Me Love You
Let Me Hold You
Let Me Show You
Let Me Free You

The Strickland Sisters Series:
Stay with Me
Believe in Me
Be with Me

The Love After Series:
Higher Love
Made to Love
Real Love

Short Stories:
Merry Christmas, Baby
Baby, Be Mine
Always My Baby

Text alexhouse to 555888 to be notified of new releases!

Made in the USA
Las Vegas, NV
22 February 2024